HER COMPASSIONATE BILLIONAIRE

JULIETTE DUNCAN

BILLIONAIRES WITH HEART CHRISTIAN ROMANCE SERIES

FOREWORD

HELLO! Thank you for choosing to read this book - I hope you enjoy it! Please note that this story is about a billionaire, Nicholas Barrington, and a grieving young woman, Phoebe Halliday, both from Australia. Australian spelling and terminology have been used and are not typos!

As a thank you for reading this book, I'd like to offer you a FREE GIFT. That's right - my FREE novella, "Hank and Sarah - A Love Story" is available exclusively to my newsletter subscribers. Go to http://www.julietteduncan.com/subscribe to get the ebook for FREE, and to be notified of future releases.

I hope you enjoy both books! Have a wonderful day!

Juliette

CHAPTER 1

Melbourne, Australia

onathan Montgomery looked up from his project blueprints and rubbed his chin, the scratch of his overnight stubble snapping him out of the daze he'd been in for what seemed hours. He fixed his gaze across Port Phillip Bay and released a deep sigh.

On the horizon, the hint of pink gave promise of yet another beautiful summer day. The view across the bay helped him focus. At ninety-five floors, Regent Towers was the tallest building in the city, and from his penthouse office he could see past the downtown skyscrapers clear across the expanse of the bay. Having this luxury made him thankful for all he had, but it hadn't always been this way. His mother would say it was by God's grace that he was now in this position, but he wasn't so sure about that. Once he would have agreed with her, but now, he wasn't certain God cared. Not since his beloved wife Larissa died.

He glanced at his watch. Six a.m. Normally his children would be rising and getting ready for school, but since they were now on their summer break, he assumed that the oldest two, Stuart and Bethany, at ten and twelve years of age respectively, would most likely still be in bed, but Molly, the youngest at seven, would no doubt be up and waking Rose, the nanny, if the woman wasn't up already.

He should have gone home last night, but there was so much to get done in such a short amount of time. Besides, that's what the nanny was there for—to care for his children when he couldn't. Like now. Tearing his gaze from the view, he returned his attention to the blueprints.

A short while later, Mrs. Shields his long-time secretary, slipped into his office almost unnoticed. For as long as he could remember, his faithful employee was in the office each morning before anyone else, her routine so perfected he barely noticed her as she moved this way and that, bringing him coffee and the morning paper with a cheery smile often accompanied by a quick admonishment if he wasn't properly caring for himself.

"Did you sleep in the office again, Mr. Montgomery?"

He feigned a scowl at the plump, pleasant woman who had been his stepfather's secretary long before he took over the reins of the family business and inherited her as his own.

"Don't bother giving me that look, sir. I know yesterday's shirt when I see it." She was possibly the only woman, aside from Larissa and his mother Peggy, who would speak to him so frankly without being intimidated.

2

Letting out a small chuckle, he shrugged and leaned back in his chair, giving her his full attention. "I didn't mean to stay so late, but I needed to make sure everything's under control with the Bayside Project." Bayside was a lower socio-economic suburb in Melbourne, and the Montgomery Corporation was committed to building not just a new community centre, but an entire neighbourhood to help improve the standard of living for the local people.

It was where Jonathon's heart in business truly lay. Giving back to the community where he'd been born and raised was the least he and his company could do.

"Your hours are not for me to judge, sir." She set a tray down on a corner of his desk. His stomach growled as the rich aroma of freshly brewed coffee filled his nostrils. "I think it's commendable you trying to get the centre open in time for Christmas. Those children deserve to have a safe, wonderful place to celebrate the birth of Jesus."

He reached for a blueberry pastry but she moved the tray out of his reach and stared him down. "But, if I may be so bold, I'd hate to see you neglect your own children in the meantime. They need their father this time of year, just as much as that community needs you, Mr. Montgomery."

He sighed heavily as she moved away and allowed him to grab the pastry, but the taste was bitter in his mouth as he absorbed her advice. Of course, she was right. His children were his world and he hated leaving them in the nanny's care for days at a time while he worked. Yet, without his philanthropic projects which absorbed so much of his time, many other children would suffer and go without.

"The children are fine. I'll head back to Seaforth shortly.

Until then, the nanny is perfectly capable of taking care of them." Even as he spoke the words, they rang hollow and a pang of guilt gnawed at his insides. The children were growing so fast and they needed more than a nanny to help them navigate the difficulties of growing up without their mother who'd lost her battle with a brain tumour four years earlier. It was always a fine line he walked between father and businessman, and he knew that too often the line blurred.

The phone on his desk rang, and before he could get to it, Mrs. Shields answered it, her face growing more pensive by the moment. His first thought was that something had happened with the project, but then he chastised himself. The call had come through on his personal line. Something must have happened to one of the children.

The phone was snug against her ear, so he could only hear Mrs. Shields' side of the conversation.

"Yes, I understand. I'll put him on, dear. And take care. We'll all be praying for you and for your father."

She covered the mouthpiece. "It's the nanny, sir. The children are fine, but her father is ill, not expected to make it past Christmas, and she has to leave immediately."

"The nanny's leaving?" Jonathon's brows drew together and he let out an exasperated sigh. What was he meant to do now?

Mrs. Shields nodded. "Yes, sir. Would you like to speak with her?" She held out the receiver. He had no choice. He took it from her and cleared his throat. "Rose, I'm sorry to hear about your father."

"Thank you, sir. And I'm so sorry to leave at such short notice. Your mother is coming over to mind the children."

"It's fine, Rose. Family comes first. When do you expect to be back?"

The line went quiet before she replied. "I...I don't think I will be coming back, sir. My mother will need me after..."

"No need to say it, Rose. I understand. It's okay. We'll manage."

"Thank you, sir. I appreciate it."

"You're more than welcome. And don't worry, Mrs. Shields will attend to your severance package." He ended the call and spun his chair around to stare out the window. The bay was now dazzling in the early morning sunshine, but his mind was elsewhere, searching for a quick solution. The phone rang again, and this time he answered it before Mrs. Shields. It was his mother.

"Jonathon. I guess you've heard?"

"Yes, I have. Rose called a few moments ago."

"I hope you were kind to her." His mother's voice bordered on condescending.

"Of course, Mother. How could I not be, under the circumstances?

"Good. Make sure you give her some extra money for the journey."

He rolled his eyes, but a smile tugged at the corners of his mouth as he covered the phone with his hand and mouthed to Mrs. Shields, "Make sure the nanny gets a nice severance package in her final pay."

The woman nodded.

He returned his attention to his mother. "Taken care of."

"Great. Now Jonathon, you know I'm more than willing to care for the children."

He tried to interrupt her but she continued talking, telling him what her plans were for the day. He appreciated her kind heart and willingness to help, but he couldn't allow her to care for all three of his children along with his stepfather who had advanced Parkinson's disease and needed almost constant care. It simply wouldn't be fair or right, even though he knew she would do it gladly.

"Let me give it some thought. I'll see what I can do to find a replacement nanny."

"This close to Christmas?"

"You never know. Miracles still happen, so I've heard." Although as the words slipped off his tongue, he wasn't so sure he believed them. There'd certainly been no miracle as far as Larissa was concerned.

After ending the call, he dropped his head into his hands, his thoughts turning to his children. They deserved so much better than he was giving them. He might have all the money in the world, but he'd gladly give it all away to have Larissa back. They needed a mother, not a replacement nanny, but since he hadn't looked at another woman since Larissa's passing, that wasn't going to happen any time soon.

He blew out a breath and raised his head. Time to get on with it. But who'd be looking for a full-time live in position so close to Christmas?

Mrs. Shields stood with her hands neatly folded in front of her, dutifully awaiting his instructions, which he proceeded to give her. "Place an advertisement immediately. I'll start interviews today."

"Right away, sir." The woman gave a nod and strode out the door.

CHAPTER 2

"*I*'m not going to be late, Mum, but I can't stand the motorway. Besides, I've plenty of time." Ruth Taylor tried her best to be patient with her mother as she drove along the arterial road hugging Port Phillip Bay on her way to the city. She was nervous enough about the interview at Regent Towers. She didn't need the aggressive motorway to make it worse. Or her mother's voice on the other end of her mobile phone.

"I know you think you do, love," her mother responded, her voice crackling on the line. "But what if there's an accident? Or something worse. I just think it'd be wise to get there as early as possible."

Ruth clenched the wheel a little tighter as she slowed for a red light. "Don't worry, Mum. I'll get there with time to spare."

"I certainly hope so. You need this job, Ruth, and I'll be praying for you the whole time."

Ruth took a breath and released it slowly. Her mother was

right. She did need this job. She'd lose the chance to buy her own home if she didn't get a job in the next few days. What bank would offer a loan to an unemployed child-care worker? None she knew of. She still couldn't believe she'd lost the job she'd held for the last fifteen years. It hadn't been her fault. The centre had closed down. Not enough children in attendance was the reason cited for its closure. And it was true. She couldn't blame the parents for shifting their children to the new Bayside Childcare Centre with its high-tech facilities and playground to die for. Goodness, if David had been a pre-schooler, she would have shifted him too. But she'd been left high and dry, with only a good reference and a month's payout after all the years she'd invested in the place. It left a sour taste in her mouth, but it was no use getting angry. God had it under control. Maybe He had other plans for her, although she'd had her heart set on one of the new affordable apartments in the Bayside Complex and had signed the purchase contract on it only days before losing her job. Now all she needed was the finance. And another job. She was tired of renting, being at the beck and call of fickle landlords. And now that David had left home to travel the world, having a place of her own had given her something to look forward to.

The position for a nanny to three young children wasn't one she'd normally consider, especially when it was a live-in job in the country, but at this time of year, with Christmas just around the corner, it was likely the only option she might have. And something about its urgency spoke to her. Three young children in need. It was as if they were calling to her.

She shook her head to dislodge the silly thought. There was most likely nothing remarkable about these children at all. It was more likely that their rich, entitled parents simply needed a regular babysitter. But still, she'd applied. The kind woman she'd spoken to had sounded relieved when Ruth confirmed she'd had experience working with young children and had even raised one of her own. No doubt the woman had been bombarded with numerous enquiries. It wasn't easy to land a job at this time of year.

"Are you still on the line, Ruthie?"

Her mother's voice snapped her out of her thoughts. Guilt at leaving her mother with dead air warmed her cheeks. How long had she let the line go silent? "Don't worry about me, Mum, I'll be fine. But I've got to go. I'll ring you as soon as the interview is over. Promise."

Ruth ended the call and concentrated on where she was going. Although she lived not far from the city, she rarely ventured out of her neighbourhood, and now as she became entangled in inner-city traffic, she began to wonder why she hadn't caught the tram. Stupid. The woman had given her instructions of where to park, and she listened intently to her navigator. She'd definitely get lost without it. After a slow crawl along three blocks, she spotted the entrance to the car park and turned in, finding a vacant spot on the third floor down. Regent Towers certainly was a massive building.

She entered via the elevators, and after being whizzed to the top floor in a glass fronted lift, she stepped into the most expansive, amazing room she'd ever seen. Marble floor tiles, lush green plants, paintings that wouldn't look out of place in an art gallery, topped off with a stunning view across the city to the bay. Wow.

A young, well-dressed receptionist smiled and directed her to take a seat. "Mr. Montgomery will be with you shortly."

Ruth's eyes widened. *Mr. Montgomery?* If Mrs. Shields had mentioned on the phone that he was the parent in need, she may not have had the nerve to follow through with the interview. She'd heard of the reclusive, billionaire developer and philanthropist. She doubted there was anyone in Melbourne who hadn't. But surely he was too old to have young children?

She eased herself carefully onto a plush leather armchair and tried to calm her racing heart as she gazed around. Windows surrounded three sides of the room, and the sleek, chrome-rimmed reception desk sat in the corner just outside a large set of smooth, polished, walnut doors she was sure led to *his* office. She gulped. What would her mother say if she got the job? Her heart rate kicked up another notch.

"Mrs. Taylor?" An older woman with a warm smile and a tight grey bun emerged from the walnut doors. *Mrs. Shields...*

"It's Ms., but that's me," Ruth said nervously as she stood, wiped her hand quickly on her black slacks, and then extended it. "Ms. Ruth Taylor, but please call me Ruth."

"Ruth it is, then. My apologies. I'm Barbara Shields, Mr. Montgomery's secretary and that of his father before him."

So that explained it. She was interviewing with the *younger* Mr. Montgomery. Of course. Ruth searched her memory for any mention in the tabloids of the son but came up empty. She'd have to go in blind.

"Mr. Montgomery is finishing up with another candidate but shouldn't be much longer." Mrs. Shields walked over to the reception desk and nodded to the woman manning the phones before turning back to Ruth. The walnut doors opened again, and a short, much younger woman, perhaps still in her late teens, walked out. On her feet were trainers and she wore what looked to Ruth like yoga pants and a sweatshirt. Not what Ruth would consider proper interview attire.

But what did one wear to an interview for a nanny's position? That morning, after leaving a pile of tried on clothes in her wake, Ruth had finally decided on a simple, lightweight pair of black slacks and a capped-sleeved dusky rose blouse. The dusky rose set off her suntanned skin, but the blouse was still modest and professional enough that she thought it would be acceptable. But who knew? Maybe the teen had it right.

The young woman turned and shook the hand of a tall, slim man who stood just inside the room. Ruth couldn't quite make out his features, but she could tell by his demeanour and smart dark grey trousers that he was a professional.

Lord, calm my nerves and go with me, and please let me know if this position is the right path for me, she prayed silently.

"Mr. Montgomery is ready for you now, Ruth." Mrs. Shields' voice broke her out of her musings just as the man turned to face her. Ruth's eyes bulged. She couldn't believe it. She knew him... She'd recognise those soulful hazel eyes anywhere. The sharply dressed, handsome, dark-haired man standing before her with his hand extended in greeting was John Robertson, her childhood crush. *Lord, what are You doing?*

"Ruth," Mrs. Shields prompted, nudging her in the side with her elbow with just enough force that Ruth let out a little cough of embarrassment.

"Oh...uh...yes." She took John's hand and despite her shock, shook it firmly. "Ruth Taylor. Pleased to meet you."

"Well, Ms. Taylor, it's a pleasure to meet you, too. I'm

Jonathon Montgomery. Would you care to come in for a quick chat?" The smooth velvet of his voice caused her stomach to flip-flop. Her childhood crush had certainly grown into an attractive man. Should she let him know she was Ruth Reynolds? Would he even remember the shy, bespectacled girl who'd followed him around like a lost puppy when they were kids?

She followed him into his office while Mrs. Shields closed the door behind them.

"Mrs. Shields said she very much enjoyed chatting with you this morning," he said, offering her the seat across from his own. A large mahogany desk sat between them and looked like it would be worth more than she could earn in a year. Things had certainly improved for John Robertson, er, Montgomery.

"She said you have experience with young children?" He leaned back in his chair and studied her.

She squeezed her hands together and forced herself to speak slowly. "Yes, I have a son who's now twenty, but I was also a childcare worker at the Mother Duck Child Care Centre in St. Kilda for the last fifteen years."

His forehead creased and he scratched his head. "St. Kilda? I grew up there."

She took a steadying breath and sat taller. Did he recognise her? Somehow she doubted it. She'd been such a quiet mouse when she was twelve. "I grew up there as well. I still live there, in fact." Suddenly her hands grew damp. This was a bad idea. How could she keep up the pretence of not knowing the man who could potentially be her employer? She should tell him.

He looked down at the portfolio in his hand and made a note in the margin before looking back at her. "Well, your C.V.

is certainly impressive." He frowned and angled his head. "You look familiar. Have we met before?"

Ruth gulped. She couldn't lie, but all of a sudden she wished the floor would open up and swallow her. As the image of John at age twelve crystallised in her mind, all those mushy feelings she'd had for him flooded back. Of course, it was simply a childhood crush, but at the time she believed she'd loved him and had even dreamt of marrying him. Her gaze flew to his left hand. At the sight of the wedding band on his third finger, an odd twinge of disappointment flowed through her. It was pure nonsense, of course, to entertain the idea that he might be mildly interested in her, either then, or now.

She released a breath and relaxed. At least that idea was put to bed. "We have," she replied, her voice steadier than she'd expected. "We went to Sunday School together as kids."

Realisation dawned across his features. He clapped his hands on the desk and his face lit up. "Ruthie Reynolds? No way, is it really you?"

"That's me," she replied with a chuckle. "But I go by Ruth Taylor now."

"Of course. Well, I go by Jonathon Montgomery these days." He swept his hands across the air as if to signal that his new last name was more about the office than anything else. "Seems we've both changed." He gave her a charming smile as he brushed his hands along the sides of his short, dark hair.

"I didn't know it was you when I applied for the position. I hope you don't think..."

"Not at all," he replied, interrupting her. "The job's yours. If you still want it."

"I do," she replied quickly. "But are you offering it to me

because of our childhood connection or because of my credentials? You've barely asked any questions."

Leaning back in his chair, he placed his hands behind his head and studied her a second before sitting forward and folding his arms on the desk. "Honestly, it's both, but I was sold on you before you came in. Your C.V. is truly impressive. The other candidate was too young and too inexperienced." He paused, took a breath. "My children are good kids, but their mother passed away four years ago and they miss her terribly. I need someone a little older and more experienced to look after them. I think you fit the bill perfectly, Ruth."

She was speechless. John was a widower? He must have loved his wife immensely to still be wearing a ring. But she needed to put all those thoughts to the side. The children were motherless, and her heart went out to them. "I'm so sorry, John. How old are the children?"

He blew out a long breath and twiddled with his pen. "Bethany's twelve, Stuart's ten, and Molly's seven." Sadness clouded his eyes and touched Ruth's heart. It was clear he missed his wife and was struggling to raise them on his own.

The idea of working for John as nanny to his three children seemed a little odd and awkward, but how could she refuse? She swallowed hard and trusted she was making the right decision. "I'd love to take the position. But I can only commit to the holiday period. Is that acceptable?"

"It'll do for now. I'm so glad you've agreed, Ruth." He visibly relaxed and smiled at her. The same smile she remembered from when they were twelve. The smile she used to dream about every night. Oh dear. Maybe this wasn't a good idea after all.

"The job starts immediately and as you know, the position is live-in. We live at Seaforth. Can you meet me there this afternoon? Let's say three p.m.? Will that give you enough time to get things in order?"

Ruth glanced at her watch. It was only ten a.m. "Sure, that's plenty of time."

"Great. Mrs. Shields will attend to all the necessaries and I'll see you this afternoon." He stood and extended his hand across the table and smiled at her again.

Dear God, help me... She took his hand and shook it, trying desperately not to think of anything other than the three children who awaited her, although deep down she sensed her world was about to change irrevocably.

CHAPTER 3

*L*ittle Ruthie Reynolds. Who would have thought? Strange how the world worked. Leaning back in his chair, Jonathon cast his mind back to his younger days. He barely remembered her from Sunday School, she was so quiet, but he did recall that she was a Godly girl, always eager to please and help when someone was in need.

He looked at her C.V. again. A childcare worker who'd raised her own child. He read between the lines and guessed she'd raised him on her own. He briefly wondered what had happened to her husband but didn't dwell on it. No doubt he'd find out in due course, although there was no real reason for him to know. The fleeting thought crossed his mind that she might be a widow. He couldn't imagine her being a divorcee. Somehow, that didn't sit right with his memory of her.

Regardless, she had experience and strength of character. He was confident he'd made the right choice.

"Mr. Montgomery?" Mrs. Shields poked her head into the office.

"Come on in, Mrs. Shields. Everything in hand with the new nanny?"

"Yes, sir. Paperwork's done and I gave her instructions of how to find Seaforth. She said she's meeting you there at three?"

"Yes. I'm taking the afternoon off, but I have a few stops to make on the way." He began shoving documents into his brief-case. "Should anything come up regarding the Christmas Eve Extravaganza in St. Kilda, push it through to my mobile."

"Are you sure, sir? Take the afternoon off and spend it with your family. We have everything covered here."

He gave the woman a warm smile. "I know, but this event is important. I want to make sure nothing slips through the cracks. Not that you'd allow that," he added quickly.

"Of course, sir."

He could count on her for all things related to the business, but how could he make her understand that he enjoyed his work? *Needed* his work? It's what kept him going. Especially the work in the communities that needed the most help. There, he could lose himself in a way he hadn't been able to with anything else since Larissa died. He'd lost his faith in everything except work. Even God. How could he explain that to her? One of the reasons his stepfather had hired her was because of her strong faith. She simply wouldn't understand his current lack.

"I'll be back first thing in the morning," he said, stuffing the last items in his case.

"Well, it's a glorious day, so enjoy the drive and your time at home. And don't hurry back." She raised a brow and looked at him sternly.

She meant to chastise but he couldn't help but chuckle. "Okay, you win. But I *will* be back tomorrow."

As he snapped his case shut and headed for the door, she stopped him. "And sir, if you don't mind me saying, you chose the right person for the position. Ruth Taylor is a keeper."

He paused before he replied, "I believe you're right, Mrs. Shields."

THE HOUR-LONG DRIVE to Seaforth was broken up by two stops along the way. One at the Bayside Development where Jonathon inspected the grounds where the Christmas Eve Extravaganza would be held. A lot of work still had to be done, but he had confidence in his team and knew that the bare earth would be transformed into a lush green oasis in time for the event. The other stop was at the Seaforth Memorial Gardens not far from his estate. Once a week he placed fresh flowers beside Larissa's memorial plaque and spent a few moments in quiet contemplation. He found the peace and quiet of the gardens a countermeasure for his busy life, but often he came away feeling more morose than when he arrived. Even after four years he felt the loss of his wife keenly and wondered when the ache in his heart would lessen.

He positioned the flowers and stared at the plaque, his thoughts turning to his wife's last days in the hospital. She'd been so brave right to the very end, an end she didn't deserve. She'd been so young. Just thirty-two. The mother of three young children. An incurable brain tumour that all the money in the world couldn't fix. He let out a long exhale. They'd had so many plans and dreams together. Now they had nothing. No. That wasn't true. There were the children. Pain still squeezed his heart whenever he thought of how much she'd loved them. She'd been a brilliant mother and they were her world. How could he even come close to filling her shoes? He couldn't. He simply couldn't.

He brushed a tear from his eye and headed back to the car and drove the short distance to his estate in silence.

Just after two o'clock, he turned into the long driveway heading up to the house. He needed to pull his focus from Larissa and place it onto the children and the new nanny who would be arriving within the hour. He needed to push away the melancholy and put on a bright face, even if it was only a façade. His children deserved better, but right now, that was all he could give them. His mother saw through it. She said he was depressed and should see someone. He told her he needed more time. The truth was, he simply didn't want to let go of his wife.

He brought the car to a halt in front of the house, drawing a steadying breath before stepping out to find his family.

THE HOUSE WAS QUIET, but that was normal. The children could be shouting at the tops of their voices in their upstairs wing and he wouldn't hear them from down here.

"Mum? Kids?" He loosened his tie and tossed it onto a hook in the hallway as he passed.

"Jonathon, is that you?" Peggy Montgomery's shrill voice called from the direction of the kitchen.

He followed his mother's voice, and reaching the large sun-filled kitchen, smiled at her. She was sitting in the breakfast nook, her face serene, barely showing a line or hint of her sixty-three years. His stepfather Mathew sat next to her. Jonathon wished he could say the same for him, but Mathew's decline over the last five years had been pronounced. The man had accepted him and his sister Janella as his own when he married their mother many years earlier, and Jonathon loved him dearly. Watching the Parkinson's slowly take over his fine motor skills had been hard on their small, tightly knit family. Now, Jonathon was humbled as he watched his mother gently feeding him, whispering sweet words of encouragement.

"I didn't expect you quite so early."

"I thought I should be here before the new nanny arrives." Jonathon walked over and gave his mother a peck on the cheek and Mathew's shoulder a squeeze.

"I sincerely hope you made a good choice." She lifted a brow and gave him a pointed look. "You know I have no problem minding the children."

"I believe I did. And yes, I know you don't, and I appreciate it, but it's better this way. Speaking of the children, where are they?"

"Cook took them down to the vegetable patch. They were excited to pick some fresh produce for their dinner tonight."

The back door flew open and Stuart and Molly rushed in, their arms overflowing with vegetables. Bethany trudged along behind them, showing far less enthusiasm than her younger siblings.

"Dad!" Stuart yelled, nearly dropping his load in the rush to greet his father.

Jonathon smiled and gave his son a hug. "Hiya, buddy. Wow, you're covered in mud."

"We were in the garden," Molly said, beaming up at him before her expression sobered. "Did you hear that Rose had to go away?"

"I did," he replied. "But not to worry. I've hired a new nanny and she'll be here soon."

"*Great,*" Bethany muttered under her breath.

"Bethany," he scolded, narrowing his eyes at his pre-teen daughter.

Pursing her lips, she folded her arms, her face stony.

"It will be all right, dear," his mother said reassuringly, patting her granddaughter's arm.

Jonathon shook his head and took a calming breath. It would be so easy to grow angry with her, but he understood to a degree how his daughter felt. In the four years since Larissa died, they'd had as many nannies. His heart went out to her, but still, there was no need for that kind of attitude. "Why don't you all go upstairs and get cleaned up? The new nanny will be here any time now. I'll show her around first and then introduce you to her when you're clean and fresh."

The two younger children put down their vegetables and rushed out of the room, shouts of excitement trailing behind them, but Bethany held back, her eyes narrowed. "I don't know why you're bothering, Dad. This one will only leave too."

Her words tore at his heart. Of the three children, she'd suffered the most as Larissa slowly slipped away, but instead of dealing with her grief with tears and talk, she'd erected barriers around her heart and had become cynical and distrusting. He wanted to help her, but how could he when he couldn't even help himself? "Let's give her a shot, shall we?"

She shrugged offhandedly before trudging up the stairs.

CHAPTER 4

*T*he drive from Ruth's apartment in St. Kilda to Seaforth would have taken just over an hour if she'd taken the motorway, but the scenic route that meandered along the bay took almost twice as long.

It had only taken an hour and a half to pack her belongings and tidy the apartment. Not that it was untidy. With David gone, everything stayed exactly the way she'd left it. She liked it that way, but it made his absence more real and highlighted the fact that she was now truly on her own for the first time in her life.

Passing through seaside towns where colourful bunting and Christmas lights criss-crossed the streets only served to remind her that this would be the first Christmas they would be spending apart, and she felt alone. For almost David's whole life, it had been only the two of them. She and Wayne Taylor had married young, but after two rough years where they fought more than they loved, he left and she ended up raising David on her own.

Her life had revolved around him, her work, her friends and her church. Now her son had packed his bags and would be spending Christmas in some far-away place, and the job she'd loved no longer existed. Only her church and her friends remained, but as she was about to start a live-in position, she wouldn't even have them for the next month or so.

Of course, God was with her, but the uncertainty of the future nibbled at her. It seemed she was at a crossroad in her life and everything she'd known until now was changing. The thought filled her with anticipation but also a little fear.

She stopped at a seaside café for a quick coffee and a bite to eat before heading east across the peninsula to Seaforth. It was only twenty kilometres to the other side, but it was a slow drive initially as the car wound its way up the narrow mountain road. Reaching the top, she paused at a lookout and gazed across the bay which was still hazy from the bush fires that had been plaguing the western side for weeks. She swiped at the flies buzzing around her head and took a sip of water from her bottle. It was going to be a long, hot summer.

Fifteen minutes later, she stopped at the bottom of the tree-lined road leading up to a whitewashed mansion on top of the hill and checked the GPS three times. This couldn't be the place. Maybe Mrs. Shields had made a mistake and given her the wrong address. But somehow, she doubted that John's efficient secretary would make a mistake like that. It had to be the place. Goodness.

Easing the clutch out, she drove slowly up the road. After a short drive through a canopy of leafy, green trees that met in the middle of the road, reminding her of an English country lane and making her feel instantly cooler, she emerged into a clearing. On her left, fences surrounded a series of well-kept, whitewashed outbuildings. Stables or horse yards, perhaps? *Did the children ride?* She'd need to brush up on her riding skills if they did. Not that she had any—there weren't many opportunities to ride in the city. Her focus shifted to the circular driveway ahead and the stunning mansion, pristine white and rising up in its surroundings like a modern-day palace. Off to the right she glimpsed a formal garden of manicured shrubs and water features, and what looked like an Olympic sized swimming pool and a path leading through another copse of trees towards the bay below.

She had, of course, guessed that John was now wealthy, but this blew her mind. With this view across the bay, the estate had to be worth millions, if not billions.

But where were the Christmas decorations? Not even a wreath adorned the front door. Where she lived, people got into the Christmas spirit early. Houses and flats all along the street were already decorated with Christmas lights and tinsel and a general sense of excitement and expectation filled the neighbourhood. But here, there was no sign of Christmas. Not an iota. How could John be so tied up with his business ventures that he'd neglect celebrating Christmas with his children? Maybe she was assuming too much. Judging him needlessly. Maybe the decorations were inside.

Parking her small sedan behind a large black SUV, she braced her arms on the steering wheel, took a deep breath and closed her eyes. *Lord, please go with me as I start this new role. Give me wisdom as I meet the children and seek to develop a rela-*

tionship with them. They must be missing their mother so much, especially at this time of year, and I feel inadequate. Not that I could ever fill that immense gap in their lives. Only You can do that, Lord, but help me to love them and show them compassion and kindness. And Lord, give me the right attitude towards John and let me not grow envious of his good fortune. I know that true joy doesn't come from material possessions and the trappings of wealth, but rather by Your good grace alone. And please help me to not think of him as anything other than my employer. I pray these things in Your dear Son's name. Amen. Calm filled her heart as she sensed the presence of God's Holy Spirit. She wasn't alone. She could do this.

Grabbing her overnight bag from the front seat, she stepped out into the warm afternoon sunshine and headed confidently to the front door.

Before she could knock, the door opened and John stood before her, the warm smile on his face making her heart flutter. *Oh Ruth. Get a grip.*

"Hello." His smile broadened as he reached for her bag. "Did you find the place okay?"

"Yes, thank you." She managed a smile. "It's quite an estate."

"Trust me, it looks way more intimidating than it is." He stepped aside, allowing her to enter the marbled foyer. "The kids are taking showers. They came in covered in mud and I thought it best they clean up before you meet them. First impressions and all." He gave a small chuckle.

Ruth couldn't imagine mud and this house going together, but the thought of the children outside playing gave her hope that despite their surroundings, they were normal kids who played and got dirty. And it was clear he was fond of them.

"Can I show you around before they come down?"

"That would be great. Thank you."

"And who do we have here?" An elegant, handsome woman with greying hair and a kind face strolled into the foyer. Dressed casually in denim and a well-ironed button-down blouse with tiny embroidered flowers across the shoulders, she carried an air of authority. Her eyes were the same hazel as John's.

"Mother, this is Ruth Reyno—Taylor, sorry." He let out an apologetic laugh. "I still can't get used to your married name."

Ruth shrugged. "It's fine."

"Ruth's the new nanny," he continued.

"Nice to meet you, Mrs. Montgomery," Ruth said, stepping forward and offering the woman her hand. She just managed to stop herself from curtseying.

"A pleasure, my dear." The older woman shook Ruth's hand firmly while looking her up and down. "Jonathon failed to mention how lovely you are. And please call me Peggy."

Ruth's cheeks warmed. "Thank you very much. You're too kind."

"Not at all. I believe in compliments when they're due."

"If you don't mind, Mum, I was just going to show Ruth around."

"Yes, of course, don't let me keep you. Your father is napping and I thought I'd attend to some correspondence while he dozes." Peggy leaned up and kissed John on the cheek before disappearing into the cavernous house.

"Your parents live here too?" she asked as she walked with John past an enormous, elegantly decorated living room. She couldn't imagine mud being welcome in this room with its off-white lounge and carpet.

"No, and Mathew is actually my stepfather. They have their own home on the grounds, but they're close enough to drop in daily, which they usually do since Larissa's been gone."

"It must be hard for you." She gulped. She hadn't intended to cross the line and speak about personal matters, but she couldn't help it. Despite his wealth, she felt sorry for him.

He stopped when they reached the kitchen and leaned his hands against the marble counter and stared out the window. Finally, he turned around, folding his arms as he spoke. "The kids have all dealt with the loss in their own ways." His voice was distant. Detached. "Molly was only three when Larissa died. To her, she's just a memory in photographs. Stuart's boisterous and full of life. He loves to tell stories about his mum before she got sick, even though his memory's shaky. He likes to keep her spirit alive with laughter. And then there's Bethany." He paused, and Ruth could hear the pain in his voice.

"She's old enough to remember," she said quietly.

John simply nodded.

Ruth immediately regretted prying. Pain squeezed her heart for the loss this family had endured, and she grew even more determined to give the best care possible to these motherless children over the Christmas holiday.

"This is a lovely kitchen," she said, changing the topic.

"Yes, it is. Larissa loved it." His voice caught.

There he went again. It seemed Bethany wasn't alone in her struggle.

Ruth would have to try harder to steer the topic of conversation away from John's wife. Not that she didn't want to hear about her, but it could become awkward if everything she said evoked memories that caused him pain.

"What other rooms are on this level?" she asked, looking around and thinking that keeping him moving might be the best approach.

"The dining room is through here," he said, pointing to a wide hallway that led from the far side of the kitchen. "We have a cook who looks after most of our meals, but feel free to help the kids with breakfast and afternoon snacks."

She nodded. Breakfast and snacks sounded easy enough.

"And out through this door are the garages. You'll have access to any of the estate's vehicles, but we also have a driver who'll be available whenever you need. Or, if you prefer, there's the Lexus SUV. I drove it today but usually it's here. Feel free to drive it whenever you wish."

The thought of driving a car worth more than her annual salary filled her with anxiety, although she wasn't about to tell John that. He obviously trusted her. She nodded and smiled. "Great. Thank you."

"You're welcome. Let's go upstairs and I'll show you your rooms."

Rooms? Plural? At best she'd hoped for a comfortable place to sleep each night, but John made it sound as if she had a suite.

She followed him up a wide, spiral staircase and once again thought she could be in a palace. The paintings adorning the walls were large, and she imagined, expensive. Possibly Monets or Van Goghs. Not that she was an art buff—far from it, but they looked like the paintings she'd studied at school. Maybe they were prints, not originals. Surely they weren't originals.

As John led her down the second-floor hallway towards her

rooms, Ruth mentally pinched herself and thanked God once again for the blessing of this position but determined that she would not allow herself to fall for John. She was his employee, and although they came from the same background, their worlds were now poles apart.

CHAPTER 5

"The children's rooms are down this hall to the left."
Jonathon was speaking quickly. He knew it. Ruth
had unsettled him. Her gentle, understanding heart had been
evident in her eyes as she listened to him talk about how each
of his children had coped with their mother's death. He could
easily have broken down and opened his heart to her, something he hadn't done with anyone since Larissa's illness had
snatched her from them.

He rarely spoke of her with anyone. He certainly didn't
allow his staff, other than Mrs. Shields, to speak on such
personal matters. But there was something about Ruth that
weakened his defences. Maybe it was because of their past.
That was probably it. She knew him before Larissa. Before all
of this.

He had to keep the tour moving. "And here on the right is
your suite."

"Suite?" Her bright blue eyes popped as he motioned for

her to step into the first of three rooms reserved for the children's caregiver, a cosy sitting area complete with two recliners, a top of the range sound system and a smart television. He could only imagine what was going through her head.

"Yes. There's a study through those doors, and the bedroom is off to your left. Feel free to make this space your own, and if there's anything you need, let one of the housekeepers, or myself know and we'll make sure you have it."

"I...I couldn't imagine needing anything more than this," she said, her voice fading to a hushed stillness.

He briefly wondered if her impoverished childhood had carried into adulthood. He didn't like the idea of her struggling when he'd lived such a privileged life, but he also didn't have the time or energy to think about why he cared. Eager to flee any emotional reaction to his new nanny and return to the business at hand, he said, "If you don't have any other questions, the children should be ready to meet you. I can show you the grounds later." He couldn't allow his history with Ruth to colour their relationship as employer and employee. He turned to re-enter the hallway when she stopped him.

"Actually, I do have a question." Her voice had regained confidence and she'd squared her shoulders.

"Yes?"

"What do you expect me to do with the children during the day now they're on summer vacation?"

Relief filled him. It was back to business. "Well, that's entirely up to you. You're basically here to do everything a mother would." He groaned inwardly. Why did he say that? "I'm sorry. Everything a full-time caregiver would."

"Yes, of course," she replied, moving past his slip-up, much to his relief. "But do they have activities or commitments over the break? Doctors' appointments? Swimming lessons?"

He frowned a moment. "I don't think they have any regular activities on now, but check the manual in the family room. Everything's in there, I believe." He felt uncomfortable standing in front of her admitting he didn't know what his children did during the day, but he'd never been involved in their day to day activities. That had always been Larissa's responsibility, and then the nanny's or his mother's.

Ruth folded her arms and pinned him with her gaze.

He felt her keen disappointment at his apparent lack of interest in his children's day to day lives. But it wasn't like that. Not really. "Sorry. I should have said that *most* of their organised activities are on break until classes resume and you should feel free to do with the children as you see fit." It was a forced recovery at best, and he hoped it satisfied her.

"Is there anything in particular they like doing?"

Jonathon scratched his head. "There's the pool, and Stuart likes riding his bike. The nanny normally looks after that type of thing. Like I said before, everything here is at your disposal, but if you want to run something by me, by all means, call me."

He led her back down the stairs where all three children were waiting. Stuart and Molly were running around after each other in the living room, but Bethany was slouching in an armchair, her feet on a footstool, flicking through her iPad.

He paused before they entered and turned to Ruth. "One more thing…"

"Yes?" Her response was polite but clipped. She was irritated with him, and he understood why. But how could he be involved in the kids' day to day lives when he was managing multi-million-dollar projects? Looking after the children was the nanny's job. He shrugged her abruptness off. It didn't matter. He was her employer and he called the shots. "Should the children call you Ms. Taylor or would you prefer to be addressed by your first name?" If she could be clipped and business-like, then so could he.

She hesitated a moment before replying, "I think it's fine if they call me Ruth." Her tone had softened again, and a hint of a grin appeared on her face. She obviously couldn't stay upset for long, and that made him smile.

CHAPTER 6

*R*uth drew a deep breath as John led her into the living room where the children were waiting. She was eager to meet them, of course. After all, they were the reason she'd accepted the position, but one glance at the eldest confirmed it wouldn't be plain sailing.

"Children, come and meet your new nanny." John waved them over. The youngest two stopped running around and hurried to stand in front of their father. Ruth didn't miss the look of contempt the older girl shot him before pushing the footstool away and standing. It was obvious she wasn't in any hurry to join them.

"Do you like animals?"

Ruth looked down and her heart lurched. The young boy, Stuart, looked up at her with his eager face, reminding her of David at that age.

"Stuart, is that how we introduce ourselves to someone

new?" John moved forward and laid a hand on the boy's shoulder.

Stuart turned bright red and shook his head before extending his hand to her. "I'm Stuart. I'm ten, and it's very nice to meet you." He quickly followed his new, more respectful introduction with, "But do you like animals? Because we have two dogs, Riley and Rex, and if you don't like animals, I don't know how we'll get on." He kept his hand extended, waiting expectantly for Ruth to take it.

She fought to suppress a smile. Except for his bright blue eyes, he looked just like John. "Well, Stuart, I'm Ruth, and it's a pleasure to make your acquaintance." She took his hand and gave it a firm shake. "As it happens, I do like animals very much and I look forward to meeting Riley and Rex. What kind of dogs are they?"

Stuart's face relaxed into an easy smile. "Golden Retrievers, and they're really good at running and swimming. Have you ever been to Australia Zoo? It's in Brisbane, and when I grow up, I'm going to work there."

"I've not been there, but I've heard about it." She glanced at John who was smiling proudly at his eager son before she returned her focus to the boy. "I bet if you study really hard, you'll be a great zookeeper. I have a son and he loves animals too. He's all grown up now."

"Has he ever been to Australia Zoo?"

"I don't think so, but he's backpacking and right now he's in the Kakadu."

"Where's that?" Stuart looked at Ruth and then at his dad.

John put his hand to his chin as if he had to think about it for a moment. "Maybe you should ask Ruth."

"Do you know, Ruth?"

"I sure do. It's at the very top of Australia."

"Wow. That's a long way." Stuart's mouth gaped.

"You're absolutely right. It's a very long way." David could have been on the other side of the world, it was that far. It certainly felt like it.

Ruth felt a tug at her side and looked down. Molly, the youngest, was tugging gently on her arm trying to get her attention. It seemed her brother's friendly enthusiasm was infectious. The girl held a doll dressed similarly to her in a blue dress, and it also had the same blonde hair and big blue eyes as her. They could almost be twins.

"And who's this?" Ruth asked, bending down to be on the same level as the child.

"Her name is Mary, and I'm Molly," the little girl said.

"Well, Molly, I think you and Mary both have very pretty names. And you look so similar. It's lovely to meet you both." Ruth offered her hand and was pleased when Molly had her shake Mary's hand first, then her own.

"I think you're very pretty," Molly said, blushing.

"Well, I think you're very pretty as well."

The girl blushed even further.

"What's your favourite colour, Molly?" Although Ruth could easily guess since both the girl and the doll were dressed in blue, she thought the question would be a good ice breaker for a seven-year-old.

"Blue," the girl said, shyly twirling around to show off her dress.

"I love blue too," Ruth said.

"Is it your favourite colour?" Molly asked.

"No, my favourite is purple, which is also the colour of my birthstone, Amethyst."

The two children stood wide-eyed, as if she'd said something profound.

Ruth couldn't help but chuckle at their innocence and exuberance. She'd half expected to find the children morose and sad but was beyond pleased to see that at least the younger two had warmed to her. She glanced at Bethany who was watching her interaction with her siblings with suspicion.

Ruth looked to John for support, hoping he'd initiate an introduction between her and the older girl, much like he had with Stuart, but he'd stepped away to take a phone call and was so involved in the conversation that he was completely unaware of the stalemate between the two of them.

She drew a slow breath. *No worries. I can handle this.* Dealing with a pre-teen girl was the thing that had concerned her most in taking this position. Boys she had experience with, thanks to David. But girls, especially girls on the cusp of their teenage years who had lost their mother, she didn't have a clue about. But God did.

She stood straighter and faced the girl. "You must be Bethany," she said, extending her hand. "I'm Ruth."

"I heard you before." Bethany ignored Ruth's outstretched hand and simply stood there, arms folded, glaring at her. "We don't need to be friends. You're just another nanny."

Feeling the sting of the girl's rejection, Ruth stiffened, momentarily abashed, but she quickly put her feelings aside. She was the adult here, and besides, she wondered how many nannies the children had had. She spoke softly. "No, we don't need to be friends, but it might be nice if we tried?"

Bethany continued to eye her suspiciously. "We'll see."

Ruth closed her eyes briefly and prayed for the special patience and wisdom that would be needed to reach the girl.

John walked back to join them, his phone call over. "Sorry about that, a quick work interruption." He smiled at everyone but quickly grew aware of Bethany's demeanour. "What did I miss?" His gaze shifted between Ruth and his daughter.

"We were just getting to know each other," Ruth said, trying to downplay the situation. She didn't want to cause the girl trouble with her father on her very first day.

"Bethany, are you behaving?" he asked anyway.

"Of course, Dad," she answered so sweetly that butter wouldn't melt in her mouth.

"Glad to hear it." John visibly relaxed. But did he truly believe her, or was he simply playing along for her sake? It was clear Bethany had no intention of behaving. "Why don't we take a walk down to the beach and show Ruth around?"

Bethany's brows shot up, puzzling Ruth. With the beach so close but John working so much, she wondered when the last time was that he had taken a walk with his children. Surely he didn't leave that to the nanny as well?

"Can we bring Rex and Riley?" Stuart pleaded. Molly joined in, jumping up and down excitedly.

John looked to Ruth and shrugged, as if silently asking her permission.

"I think bringing the dogs would be a great way for me to get to know them too," she replied, frowning at him. Why would he need her approval to take the dogs? Did he not have much to do with them, either?

"Then it's settled. Stu, go get the animals and we'll leave

right away." John scooped Molly up and placed her on his shoulders, much to her delight and Ruth's surprise.

Ruth glanced back at Bethany who was dragging her feet but nevertheless, was following. A walk was a great idea. Maybe she'd get some time alone with Bethany along the way, and the chance to break the ice with her. Although, to be honest, she felt totally inadequate and out of her depth with the pre-teen. What on earth had made her think she could do this?

CHAPTER 7

"Wait, Dad. Put me down!" Molly started squirming and wriggling on Jonathon's shoulders. Having barely made it out the door, he couldn't for the life of him figure out what had made his youngest daughter want to desperately head back inside.

Setting her down, he asked what was wrong, but she sprinted inside the house without answering. Frowning, he scratched his head.

"Maybe she had to use the toilet," Ruth said quietly. "Should I go check?"

Before he had a chance to answer, Molly had returned, out of breath but smiling broadly.

"What was that all about, sweetheart?" he asked.

"I forgot Mary." She beamed at him as she held her doll up for his inspection.

"We can't have a walk to the beach without Mary, can we?" He leaned down and scooped her up, and as he did, he caught

Ruth's gaze which was filled with warmth and mirth. He could already tell she was developing a soft spot for Molly, and that pleased him greatly. He gave his daughter a tight hug that she returned before he hoisted her onto his shoulders again.

After a kilometre of tree-lined estate road, the asphalt stopped and the gravel started. Manicured trees morphed into native bushland and the road narrowed to a trail that led all the way to the beach. When he and Larissa were looking to build their dream home, they'd specifically wanted land that led down to this part of the bay. With Point Leopold in the distance and a wide expanse of soft sand leading out to crystal blue water, it was the perfect place to call home.

The sea breeze hit his face while familiar sights and smells assaulted him. How long had it been since he'd taken the time to walk to the beach? He knew that Rose, the previous nanny, had often brought the children down. Many nights when he arrived home, the aroma of coconut sun cream wafted in the air. Now, watching the ease with which Stuart and Molly ambled along the trail, he guessed they were as familiar with this stretch of beach as he used to be.

Jonathon allowed his mind to wander back to the last family walk they'd taken together. Larissa had barely been strong enough to keep her legs moving and he'd supported her with his own strength as Bethany ran ahead and tried to make her laugh. He glanced back at Bethany now, so quiet and pensive as she lagged behind, and his heart broke for her.

"She needs time," Ruth said, as if reading his mind.

So wrapped in his thoughts, he hadn't noticed she was walking beside him. He blew out a heavy breath. "I know. I only wish I knew how much she needs. It's already been four years. I hate seeing her like this."

"Dad!" Stuart came running up, with Molly and the two dogs in tow. "We should go to Point Leopold for ice cream!"

"Yes!" Molly agreed with a squeal. The dogs, drenched from splashing in the water, stopped in front of them and shook, sending spray over everyone.

Jonathon chuckled. He should have known that by coming down to the beach there'd be no way his children would be able to resist asking for a treat when the yacht club and café were so close. "There's still an hour or so before dinner, so I guess it wouldn't hurt too much, but what does our new nanny think?"

"Oh, I don't know..." Ruth tapped her index finger against her chin.

"Oh, please, Ruth," Molly begged, her hands together as if she were praying.

"Yes, please, they have *the* best ice cream," Stuart added.

"*The* best ice cream, huh? Really? In all of Seaforth?" She played along.

"In all the world!" Stuart said.

Jonathon couldn't help but chuckle at the boy's emphatic support of the cafe's ice cream quality. He watched as the children danced around Ruth begging her to say yes. Even Bethany stood close by with what looked like a vested interest in Ruth's nanny's response.

"What do you think, Bethany?" Ruth asked.

"It's good, I guess." She shrugged but sounded reasonably polite. It was the most she'd said since they'd left the house, and Jonathon began to hope that perhaps Ruth could reach his daughter when no one else had been able to. Not even his mother.

"Well, that settles it. If everyone promises to eat all their dinner, I guess having an ice cream is acceptable. After all, it *is* the best." Ruth winked at Stuart, making him laugh.

"If Ruth agrees, then who am I to argue?" Jonathon added.

Molly and Stuart jumped up and down cheering, and even Rex and Riley joined in the excitement with boisterous barking.

They strolled slowly along the foreshore towards the café, although Stuart and Molly kept running ahead with the dogs and then had to wait for the adults and Bethany, to catch up. Jonathon was very aware of Ruth walking beside him, but couldn't shake the memory of similar walks with Larissa.

The small café bustled with locals and tourists warding off the late afternoon heat with ice creams and cool drinks. They lined up and the girl behind the counter patiently took their orders. Stuart chose chocolate, Molly strawberry, Bethany cookies and cream, and Jonathon and Ruth both chose butterscotch.

Immediately after finishing his, Stuart and the dogs sprinted to the rock pools where a bunch of children of a similar age were playing. Jonathon thought he recognised some of the boys from his son's football team, but wasn't sure.

Molly was sitting on Ruth's lap finishing her cone while playing with her doll. She'd taken to the new nanny so quickly, and it confirmed to Jonathon that he'd made the right decision in choosing Ruth. She had the right mind-set and intelligence to deal with his children, even Bethany. The fact that they knew each other as children only made him more comfortable trusting her around his own.

He turned his gaze from Molly to Bethany, who was sitting alone on a rock on the edge of the beach, staring out across the bay, her arms wrapped around her drawn up legs. She looked so much like her mother it brought a lump to his throat. Larissa had struck the same pose on those very rocks whenever she'd been deep in thought. It was unbelievable how much he missed her.

"What do you think she's looking at?" Ruth asked.

"I'm not sure. She seems to be staring at nothing."

"That's what I thought initially, but I think she's watching that surfing class." Ruth pointed out past the breaks and sure enough, someone, probably the instructor, was sitting on a surfboard facing a row of novice surfers.

"I think you're right. But she's never shown any interest in surfing." In fact, of late, she hadn't seemed interested in anything other than her iPad. If only he could reach her, but he didn't know how. How was it he could haggle with the toughest of negotiators, but he couldn't talk with his own daughter? It grieved him, but he also knew that if he did break through her hardened exterior, his own grief would also be exposed, and honestly, that scared him.

"Lots of kids develop interests at her age. David was twelve when he grew interested in hiking and camping."

"I guess that makes sense. But surfing? I don't think so. She's probably just staring into the distance." He took the last bite of his ice cream and changed the topic. "You must miss your son."

"Yes. David's leaving was hard. It had been only the two of

us for so long, and then, in the blink of an eye, he wasn't my little boy anymore. He was a man, going off on his own. I guess I was naïve thinking the day would never come."

"They grow up so fast."

"They really do. Sometimes I wish he was my little boy again." She drew a slow breath and looked at him.

As their gazes met, an image of little Ruthie Reynolds danced before his eyes. It seemed like just yesterday that they were twelve.

"Don't get me wrong," she continued. "I'm so proud of the man he's become, and I'm excited for his future. But sometimes I wish he was Molly's age again and that we could spend more time together."

At the mention of her name, Molly looked up and flashed him a bright smile, looking very cute with her two missing front teeth. Ruth was right. Time passed all too quickly and his children, especially Bethany, would be grown up before he knew it. It was happening already. If only Larissa was here to help him navigate these unchartered waters.

Suddenly overwhelmed by the emotion and memories that had been stirred inside him, Jonathon stood and whistled for the other children and the dogs. He needed to get home and bury himself in work, the only place he could hide from the memories and pain.

Rex and Riley stopped digging in the sand and trotted back. Stuart and Bethany looked his way. "We need to head home, it's getting late," he yelled.

While the two older children made their way back, Ruth helped Molly finish braiding Mary's hair. From the occasional glance she shot him, he could tell his change of mood confused her. But it was too much. It was all too much.

Heading back up the track, he gazed out at a line of dark clouds forming on the horizon across the bay. A storm was brewing, and he sensed it wasn't just a physical one.

CHAPTER 8

*J*ohn, Stuart and Molly walked ahead as they all made their way back to the house, while Rex and Riley had to constantly be called back as they darted here and there, sniffing and smelling everything in their path.

Ruth hung back, choosing to keep pace with Bethany who was lagging behind. "Did you have fun at the beach?" she asked as they strolled along. A crack of thunder in the distance made her wonder if they shouldn't be walking a little faster.

"It was all right, I guess." Bethany shrugged.

"I noticed you staring out across the water. Is everything okay?"

"You don't have to try and be my friend, you know."

"I know I don't *have* to try." Bethany's harsh tone didn't offend Ruth and her reply was soft and caring. She couldn't imagine what it would be like to be entering puberty without a mother and her heart went out to the girl. "I'm genuinely interested, that's all."

Bethany shrugged again and turned her head away. The conversation was over. Ruth tried not to feel defeated. It was only her first day. She wondered what Bethany's relationship was like with her grandmother. Peggy seemed a wise woman, and often grandmothers had a special way with their grandchildren. Still, twelve was a confusing and angst-ridden time in any girl's life. Would either of them be able to help compensate for her not having her mother's love and understanding that she obviously longed for? She prayed silently for the girl as they walked along together. *Oh Lord, please help me navigate these waters and let Bethany see that only You can heal her hurting heart.*

REACHING THE HOUSE, the most amazing aromas greeted Ruth as she set foot in the door. Her stomach growled as she realised how hungry she was. It must have been the fresh air. She closed her eyes as the aromatic smell of rosemary and roasting meats tickled her nose.

"All right, kids, go wash up and get ready for dinner," John told the children, although Stuart and Molly were already halfway up the stairs. After Bethany followed them, he spoke to Ruth. "You're welcome to join us for dinner if you wish, or if you prefer, you can eat in the kitchen. Or in your room. Whatever you like. I'm not often home for dinner, but when I am, we usually eat in the dining room together."

She hesitated. Eating with John and the children almost seemed like overstepping an imaginary line. She was an employee. A nanny. Eating with the children when he wasn't home was one thing, but when he was here? She thought of one of her favourite television shows, Downton Abbey. The nanny would never have dreamt of eating with the family at their dining table. But this was different. This was John, and he'd told her she was welcome to join them.

"Dad…the nanny should eat in the kitchen." Bethany had stopped halfway up the stairs, her jaw tight as she glared first at her father and then at Ruth.

"Bethany," John snapped. It was the closest Ruth had heard him sounding cross, and she felt bad that it was on her behalf. "Apologise to Ruth. She has every right to enjoy a family meal with us on her first night."

"It's all right," Ruth said, knowing better than to take offence at the girl's protest. Bethany was wary of new people, she hadn't exactly warmed to her yet, and she was protective of her father. "I'd actually prefer to take a plate to my room tonight, if you don't mind. I have a few calls to make."

"Are you sure? You're more than welcome." By the way he looked at her she was sure he'd guessed she wasn't being entirely truthful. He wasn't far off, but it wasn't exactly a lie. She detested even half-truths and avoided them whenever she could, yet she felt in this case it was better for Bethany if she took her dinner alone, especially since John had admitted that he wasn't home in the evenings as much as the children would like him to be. She'd have plenty of opportunities to share meals with them, anyway.

"I'm sure," she replied. "I'll head to the kitchen and introduce myself to the cook and grab a plate."

"Okay, but I'll need help with putting the children to bed a little later."

She nodded. "That won't be a problem. Call me when you're ready."

Leaving John, she made her way through the house to the kitchen, the delicious smells becoming more pronounced the closer she got. Ruth paused when she reached the large, well-appointed kitchen. A tall woman wearing a traditional chef's coat stood with her back to her, carving meat.

"Hello…" Ruth called out softly.

The woman turned. Wisps of grey hair poked out from under her cap, making her look older than Ruth had initially thought she was. "You must be the new nanny!" she said, her smile wide and genuine.

Ruth instantly knew she was going to like her. "Yes, Ruth Taylor. Pleased to meet you." She extended a hand in greeting.

"Madeline Waters," the woman replied, wiping her hands on a towel kept at her side, and returning Ruth's handshake with a solid grip. "Have you eaten?"

"Not yet, but everything smells wonderful."

"Thank you. I knew Mr. Montgomery would be home tonight so I made a special roast, one of his favourites."

Ruth saw the respect the cook had for John in her eyes. That was a good thing. He must treat his staff well. Not that she had any reason to believe he didn't. Still, it felt nice to see her initial opinions corroborated in others. She thought back on the kind and thoughtful boy he'd been, always helping those who needed it and befriending the boys in Sunday School whom no one else could be bothered with. It seemed he'd brought some of those qualities into adulthood.

Madeline motioned for her to sit at the island and set a plate piled high with roast meat, crispy baked potatoes, vegetables and gravy in front of her. Usually Ruth wouldn't eat such a large meal, but she was starving after their long walk and getting acclimated to her new role.

"This looks amazing," she said as she dug right in, thoughts of going to her room and eating alone having gone by the wayside. The first bite was so delectable she closed her eyes and moaned as she chewed. It was possibly the best meal she'd ever eaten. "Wow."

"I think we'll be friends, Ruth Taylor," Madeline chuckled as she returned to her carving.

Ruth smiled. Madeline wasn't only a genius with food, she also seemed a nice woman. "I think you're right. I think we'll be great friends," she replied after swallowing another mouthful. A friend in the house would be nice. A friend in the house who cooked like a Michelin starred chef would be wonderful.

CHAPTER 9

*A*lthough Jonathon had been determined to lose himself in his work after the walk to the beach, Ruth's words had haunted him and he decided to leave the work until later. He needed to enjoy dinner with the children, regardless of how he felt.

Now, seated at the dining table with them, the youngest two chatted in between mouthfuls, telling him about this and that, but Bethany was conspicuously silent after her earlier outburst.

"How's your dinner, Bethie?" He used her childhood nickname, hoping to at least get a smile.

She shrugged as she picked at a roasted potato. "It's all right."

"Just all right?"

"I mean, it's good. But Madeline always makes good food." She gave another non-committal shrug.

He let out an exasperated sigh. Instead of trying to drag

more adjectives out of his pre-teen, he changed the subject. "So, what do you guys think of Ruth?" He set his fork down and joined his hands together, placing his chin on them as he shifted his gaze between each of his children.

"I like her a lot." Molly's smile was like a sunbeam, bright and warm.

"Yeah, she's great," Stuart added. "Plus, she likes animals. I mean, I'm gonna miss Rose, but she didn't love Rex and Riley. I don't think she even liked them. Not like Ruth does."

It gladdened him that at least two of his children had taken to Ruth. Although she resembled the shy girl he remembered from his childhood, she'd also changed, gaining confidence and wisdom, something he found comforting if not a little confronting.

"She's okay, I guess," Bethany mumbled.

Before he could ask her to elaborate, his phone rang. He wanted to ignore it, but it was most likely important. The name flashing on the screen was Gareth, the project manager in charge of handling the logistics of the Bayside Christmas Eve Extravaganza. Jonathon groaned. Something had to be wrong for him to be calling. "I'm sorry, guys, I've gotta take this." He looked up, readying himself for the disappointment in his children's eyes.

At that exact moment, Ruth poked her head into the room and asked the children if they'd finished their dinner.

His brows arched in surprise.

She simply lifted a shoulder and gave a short nod. How she'd heard the phone ring from her room was a mystery, but he was glad she'd come to his rescue.

"If you've finished, I'd love to see your rooms," she said to the children.

He nodded his appreciation before leaving to take the call.

"LET me show you my room first!" Molly jumped up from the table and grabbed Ruth's hand.

Ruth laughed. "Okay, but slow down! We need to wait for the other two." She glanced at Bethany and groaned at the hostility in the pre-teen's eyes. How was she ever going to get through to her?

"Come on, you two. Show me your rooms." She smiled at Stuart and Bethany and waited for them to stand before directing them to go ahead. She followed them upstairs with Molly chattering beside her the entire time, reminding Ruth of one of the little girls from her Sunday School class. Trudie's mother had been worried about her daughter when she was little because she was slow to start talking, but now, at seven years of age, she never stopped. Much like Molly. She was a delightful child. So innocent. So loving. Knowing the loss she'd suffered when she was so young, it was difficult to understand how she was so content and happy. Ruth could only think that she felt loved and secure, even though her father was more absent than present from what she'd gathered already.

Stuart and Bethany hovered in the hallway while Molly exuberantly showed Ruth her room, which was simply delight-ful. An entire family of fluffy animals was piled on her four-poster bed which was draped with a soft-pink canopy. What looked like a hand-made doll house, complete with miniature furniture on all three levels, filled one corner. Ruth wondered who had made it for her. John? Perhaps his stepfather? And who had decorated the room? Peggy, or one of the nannies? Whoever it had been, they'd done a wonderful job.

"This is a lovely room, Molly. It's beautiful."

Her little face lit up even more. "Thank you! Can you read to me before bed?"

Ruth smiled. "I'd love to. But before we do that, I need to look at Stuart and Bethany's rooms."

"Okay." She skipped off happily towards the door, grabbing Ruth's hand on the way, a sweet gesture that suddenly brought a lump to Ruth's throat.

Stuart showed her his room next. It was a typical ten-year-old boy's room with race cars and transformers spilling out of a large plastic toy box on the floor, and a more practical bed than Molly's. The walls were covered with posters of mountain bikes and football players. There was no doubting what interested him.

Next was Bethany's room. Suddenly, Ruth felt as though she was entering the girl's private world and almost suggested it wasn't necessary for her to view it. But Molly dragged her in before she could say anything. "Bethie has a messy room," she announced, taunting her sister.

Bethany kept her expression neutral and didn't react, but Ruth had to agree, her room was indeed messy. Clothes were strewn all over the floor and her bed was unmade. Ruth assumed there would have been a maid who cleaned up every day, but perhaps not. Or else, Bethany had recently made this mess, possibly for Ruth's benefit. Other than the obvious mess, her walls were filled with posters of pop stars and animals, but what caught Ruth's attention the most was the photograph on top of the bookshelf of Bethany holding a woman's hand. *Larissa. John's wife.* It had obviously been taken before she grew sick because she looked a picture of health. Smiling, happy, content, as did Bethany. It seemed so unfair. Ruth didn't usually question God. She knew better than that, but at times like this it was difficult not to. She swallowed the lump in her throat and smiled at Bethany. Somehow, she felt her reason for being here was to help this motherless pre-teen, but oh goodness, was she out of her comfort zone. She desperately needed wisdom from above. "It's a nice room, Bethany. And I don't care about the mess."

Ruth thought she saw a tear form in the girl's eye, but she wasn't sure because she quickly flopped onto her bed. "I'm going to read for a while," she said, hiding her face in a magazine she grabbed from the floor.

"Okay, that's fine." Ruth smiled again and stepped back to the hallway. Stuart had stayed in his room and was playing with his racing cars. She turned to Molly who'd sprinted to her room and returned holding a book of Bible stories.

"Will you read me a story now?" she asked in such a sweet voice Ruth couldn't deny her, even if she wanted to.

"Of course, sweetheart. Why don't we go back to your room and get your pjs on first? Then I'll read you three stories."

"Three? You promise?"

Ruth nodded. "Yes. I promise I'll read three stories."

Cuddled up with Molly on her four-poster bed surrounded by pink tulle and princess pillows reminded Ruth of how she'd longed for a little girl of her own. She wouldn't trade her

David for anything, but she had to admit there was something special about a little girl. Especially one as cute as Molly.

True to her word, she read Molly three of her favourite stories from the big book. *Joseph and His Coat of Many Colours* was Ruth's favourite, while Molly preferred the story of *Daniel in the Lion's Den.* They both decided that *Noah and his Ark* was also good, but not as fun and exciting as the other two.

"Will you stay while I say my prayers?"

Once again, Ruth felt powerless to refuse such a heartfelt request. Nor did she want to. "Of course I will," she replied.

As Molly knelt and folded her small hands, Ruth's heart clenched. The sweet girl must have learned to pray from someone. She was much too young for her mother to have taught her. Had it been the previous nannies or Peggy who'd instilled faith in the child? Or could it be that Molly had learned to pray from her father? Ruth wasn't sure if John had kept his faith or not, but perhaps he had.

"Please, dear God," Molly began. "Keep my mummy safe in heaven, and watch over my Grandma and Papa, and look after Daddy. I know he doesn't pray as much as he should, but he's a good daddy. And also, thank You for bringing Ruth to us. I like her a lot. Amen."

Ruth opened her eyes but quickly shut them again as Molly re-clasped her hands and continued. "Oh... and God, please look after Mary. Amen."

Ruth chuckled at the little girl's innocence. "Let's get you into bed," she said when it was clear Molly was satisfied with her prayers.

Molly climbed up and snuggled under the bed covers. Ruth tickled her and Molly let out a peel of giggles that Ruth answered in kind. She found Mary on the floor next to the bed and tucked the doll in beside the little girl. "Is there anything else you need before you go to sleep?"

Molly played with Mary's hair and then looked up. "No, but can I ask you something?"

"Sure, sweetheart. What is it?"

"Will you promise to stay longer than Rose and the others?"

Oh goodness. What a question. How could she promise to stay when she had her heart set on getting her own apartment? How could she tell this sweet little girl that she only intended to stay until the holiday was over?

She swallowed hard and ran a gentle hand across the girl's forehead, pushing a lock of fine blonde hair off her cheek before planting a kiss on her forehead. "Oh darling, that's so sweet, but it's only my first day. How about you ask me in a week's time?"

Molly nodded and her eyelids began to droop.

Ruth could only pray that she would have forgotten the request by then.

CHAPTER 10

*J*onathon disconnected the phone call and raked his hand across his hair. How could the caterer cancel this close to the event when they'd been booked for so long? Was it a conspiracy? First the nanny, now the caterer?

Groaning, he looked around his desk for his Bayside binder. It had to be here somewhere. He needed to get a replacement list of potential caterers to his team as quickly as possible. Otherwise there'd be no food at the Extravaganza. He couldn't trust Gareth his project manager to get it done without his overseeing the details. He wouldn't have called Jonathon on his mobile during dinner if he'd been able to handle it.

Where was it? Surely he hadn't left it at the office. He wouldn't have done that. No, it must be in the car.

As he hurried through the house to the front door, sounds of laughter drifted down the stairs and he paused to listen. It sounded like Molly and Ruth were getting along well, and that pleased him. No matter how much of a challenge the Bayside Christmas Eve Extravaganza was becoming, at least he'd hit the jackpot with the replacement nanny.

He couldn't remember the last time he'd heard a woman's laughter in the house, and he realised with a start that he missed it. His heart clenched once again as memories of Larissa flooded back. Her dying so young was grossly unfair. He sighed heavily and headed outside. Life went on, he knew that, and tonight, he had work to do. There was no time for self-pity and moroseness.

AFTER SUCCESSFULLY GETTING Molly to sleep and checking on Stuart and Bethany, Ruth headed downstairs to speak with John before retiring for the night. She wanted to learn more about his schedule, and even though he'd told her she had free rein with the children, she wanted to talk to him further about what that meant.

The living areas and kitchen were shrouded in darkness and the cavernous house felt less like a home and more like a hotel. *It could definitely use a touch of warmth,* Ruth thought as she made her way down one of the ground-floor hallways. John had told her his study was on that level, and she guessed that's where he'd ended up after he took the phone call she'd heard from the kitchen while she was eating dinner. It was only nine o'clock. Much too early for him to have gone to bed.

Soft music sounded from the end of the hallway. She couldn't quite make it out, but it sounded an awful lot like

Christmas music which surprised her since there were no decorations inside the house either. She walked along the hallway, taking note of the artwork lit up by fancy wall sconces that lined the walls, until she reached a door that was slightly ajar and had light spilling out from it.

She peered in, not at all surprised to see John leaning over his large walnut desk, head in hands pouring over a thick three-ring binder. Not wanting to startle him, she gave a light knock on the door. "Hello. Is everything all right?"

Looking up, he released a tired sigh. "I'm not sure."

"Would you like to talk about it?" She still had her own agenda, but maybe now wasn't the right time. He seemed to have pressing matters consuming his attention.

He leaned back in his chair and placed his hands behind his head. He looked handsomely rugged with his shirt sleeves rolled up and a day's stubble dusting his chin.

"It depends. What do you know about the new Bayside development?"

Her eyes widened. "The…the new housing and community centre off Bayside Road?"

"That's the one."

She gulped. *Don't tell me he owns the very development where I'm planning to live.* She slipped into the room and perched on the oversized leather chair facing his desk.

"We're opening to the public week after next, and we're hosting a free Christmas Extravaganza there on Christmas Eve, much like the ones we used to have when we were kids. Do you remember them? Carols by candlelight, a funfair, loads of food and ice cream. And of course, a visit by Santa, although I want the focus to be on the true meaning of Christmas."

Wow. She'd planned to go to the Extravaganza with a girl-friend, but her new job had thrown those plans out the window. She nodded. "Yes, I remember." How could she forget? Especially the ones when she'd followed him around like a love-sick puppy. But he wouldn't remember that. He probably hadn't even been aware she was there. "I'd heard the event was happening this year and had planned to go to it," she finally replied.

"Really?"

She nodded again.

"It's a small world."

Not nearly as small as you think...

"Why don't you still come and bring the children? It'll be a lot of fun."

Hmmm... That meant he hadn't been planning to spend Christmas Eve with his own family. "Okay..." She narrowed her eyes. "But what's got you worried?"

He groaned. "We just lost the caterer."

"Two weeks before Christmas?"

"Yep."

"Is there anything I can do to help?"

"That's kind of you to ask, but don't worry yourself. I've got an entire team working on the party and I've already given the project manager a list of caterers to contact. We'll be back on track in no time."

"Well, if you need anything..." She stood to take her leave, her own agenda temporarily forgotten.

"Thank you. I'll keep that in mind." Their gazes met and his compelling eyes riveted her to the spot. There was something tangible between them. Maybe it was simply their past connection, but if she were honest, her infatuation as a twelve-year-old with John Robertson was quickly resurfacing.

"Do you remember how to get to your rooms, or would you like me to walk with you?"

Her heart thumped faster. It was a tempting offer. But no, she knew the way. And besides, she needed to calm her heart. "Thanks, but I think I can remember."

"I hope you sleep well in your new surroundings. Good-night, Ruth."

"Goodnight, John." She gave him a smile as she made her way out of his office into the hallway, her heart heaving. Slumping against the wall, she closed her eyes. He'd grown into such a handsome and kind man. If she wasn't careful, she'd soon be falling in love with him. If she hadn't already.

CHAPTER 11

*R*uth and the children hadn't seen John in almost two days. He'd left for the office each morning before they woke and didn't return until long after the household had settled in each night. His long hours worried her. She could see how much the children missed him, and she fully intended to speak with him when she saw him next.

She was pleased, however, with the routine they'd begun to settle into. Even Bethany had started to warm towards her, if only a little. Still, it was progress and gave Ruth hope.

On the third morning, when Ruth and Bethany were sitting at the breakfast bar alone, Stuart and Molly both having raced outside to pat the dogs before having theirs, Ruth took the opportunity to speak with her. "Is there anything special you'd like to do these holidays, Bethany?"

The girl looked up and raised a brow, as if taunting her. "Do you really want to know?"

Ruth nodded. "I do, or I wouldn't have asked."

The corner of Bethany's lip twitched and she fixed her gaze on the cereal packet in the middle of the table. When she spoke, her voice was so quiet Ruth wasn't sure she heard her correctly when she said, "I want to take surfing lessons."

"Sorry. Did you say surfing lessons?"

Bethany pulled her gaze from the cereal packet and held Ruth's. "Yes."

"I think that's wonderful!" Ruth wanted to lean over and squeeze her in a tight embrace but thought better of it. But her heart swelled. That Bethany had trusted her enough to share this was a real breakthrough.

"Really? You do?" Bethany's eyes widened.

"Really and truly. Have you told your father?"

She looked down and fiddled with her hands. "No, he'd probably just say it's silly." She seemed to already be defeated, and Ruth winced with the pain she felt radiating from Bethany. But why would she be so hesitant to ask her father? Ruth hadn't detected any real problem between the two, other than the fact that John was rarely at home.

"I'll talk to him about it if you like." Surely John would be eager to allow his daughter to do an activity that involved sunshine and water. It had to be better than her being on her iPad all day.

"Would you?" Bethany's expression brightened with hope, and Ruth nodded quickly before Stuart and Molly raced into the kitchen and jumped on their stools.

"Do we have to have cereal again?" Stuart had enough of a whine in his voice to earn a pointed look from Ruth.

"Cereal during the week, you know that," she replied. "Weekends are for special treats like pancakes and bacon."

He immediately flashed a bright smile and took a large sip of his orange juice. Breakfast had quickly turned into Ruth's favourite time in the Montgomery house. Madeline didn't arrive until later in the morning, so it was her responsibility to ensure the children were fed, and she enjoyed spending the time with them as they ate their cereal and toast.

"I like cereal," Molly chimed in, never missing an opportunity to appear better than her brother.

"You like everything," Bethany added, snidely.

"All right, then, no more of that." Ruth clapped her hands and looked out the large bay window onto the beautifully manicured lawn. "So, what shall we do today?"

"I want to go riding with Dwayne," Stuart said through a large milky bite of his cereal.

Ruth searched her memory for who Dwayne was and came to the conclusion that she needed to consult the instruction manual. As much as she found an instruction manual for children to be a laughable idea, when it came to lists of their friends and activities they enjoyed and were allowed to participate in, it was rather helpful. Turning to Stuart's pages while he ate, she found it was indeed okay for him to go bike riding with Dwayne. The boy lived in the neighbourhood and his family's estate shared common paths with the Montgomery estate.

"Okay then, you can go riding with your friend. But no crossing the main road. Stick to the paths between the houses."

He jumped up from the table, quickly putting his dish into the sink, and ran out the door in a flash. Ruth shook her head and laughed before turning to the girls. "All right, it's just us three. What shall we do today?"

Bethany shrugged. "It doesn't matter what we do, it's going to be boring."

Ruth sighed. One step forward, two back, it seemed. Before she could stop herself, she tossed the older girl a stern look but immediately regretted it. Maybe that wasn't the way to go about getting close to Bethany.

"What do you think we should do, Ruth?" Molly asked before Ruth could say anything further.

She placed her hand on her chin and played hard at pretending to think. "Well," she finally answered, "how about we put up a Christmas tree and decorate the house for Christmas?"

Both girls' eyes lit up. "Rose said it would be too much trouble," Bethany said, "so we forgot about it."

"Too much trouble to decorate for Christmas? Not at all! It's the most wonderful time of year!" Why would anyone think it was too much trouble? Ruth was aghast that her predecessor had thought that, but then perhaps her mind had been elsewhere... with her sick father. She could understand how difficult it would be to be excited about Christmas decorations when your father was so unwell.

"Let's get dressed for the day, shall we, and then we can head to the stores and get all the decorations we need."

The two girls exchanged a knowing glance. "We don't need to go shopping," Bethany said.

"Of course we do," Ruth replied, suddenly excited with the idea of bringing some Christmas cheer into the Montgomery house. "How else will we get the items we need to trim the tree? We need tinsel and ornaments. We can make some, I guess, oh, and of course, we need a tree—"

"No, you don't understand," Bethany said again, hands on her hips as she stopped Ruth's rapid-fire train of thought in the middle of her list making. "We have a tree. We have two as a matter of fact."

"Yeah," Molly said. "And we have boxes and boxes of decorations in the garage. I've seen them."

"Okay. Let's go. Show me."

The girls were right. There was indeed a plethora of boxes containing Christmas decorations in the garage storage area. She looked for one that might contain the tree, and finally came across two long cardboard boxes with sturdy plastic handles running along one side, labelled 'Tree'. Ruth struggled to get them down from the top shelf and was pleased when Bethany offered to help.

Once the boxes were on the floor, she straightened and wiped the sweat from her brow. She and the girls had been digging out boxes labelled Christmas for over an hour, and now, having found the trees, she was satisfied with what they'd discovered. There'd be enough lights and decorations to bring a truckload of holiday cheer to the Montgomery house.

More than once, Ruth glanced outside and noticed Stuart and his friend Dwayne craning their necks over the handlebars of their bikes to see what the girls were up to. She was pleased that he'd listened to her and had stayed around the paths on the property.

"We're going to start trimming the tree if you and your friend would like to come," she called out the next time they passed. "Madeline's making iced chocolate with marshmallows as well." Ruth couldn't help but smile at the look the two boys exchanged. Bicycles quickly forgotten, they sprinted to join the girls in the house.

Soon, with Christmas carols playing on the sound system, Ruth and the children became engrossed with decorating the tree with lights and tinsel. Finally it was time to add the baubles and ornaments.

"Ah hah!" she said, crawling over a few empty boxes to locate one she'd seen earlier that had the word 'ornaments' written on it. "I knew I'd seen it." She opened the box and held up a few handmade ones for everyone to see.

"We made those!" Stuart exclaimed.

Ruth looked carefully at each ornament as she unwrapped them from their newspaper rolls. "I can tell. They're lovely," she said, turning over a small plaster ornament with what looked like an imprint of a chubby, toddler's hand, painted red and green in the sloppy, loving way that only a child could do.

Bethany walked over and picked a similar one up, rolling it gently back and forth in her hand. She seemed to be contemplating saying something and Ruth immediately knew why.

"Did you make that with your mum?" she asked softly. She didn't want to upset the girl, but she also wanted her to know it was okay, and even nice, to talk about her mother.

"It was the Christmas before she, before she—"

"Before God called your mother home?" Ruth supplied, gently taking the small round plaster ball from Bethany's hand to look at.

"No," Bethany said, swiping a stray tear that had begun to fall, her stoic bravery firmly back in place as she snatched the ornament back from Ruth. "God didn't take Mum anywhere.

She died. God isn't real, just like Santa isn't real. It's all made up!"

"Oh, Bethany. God *is* real. And He loves you and He loves your mother so very much."

"If He were real, He wouldn't have let her get sick and die." Her voice was flat, determined. "God never loved me. If He did, my mum would be here now, instead of you."

Ouch. Bethany's words stung, but the hurt in her voice squeezed Ruth's heart until it ached. She was sure Bethany didn't believe what she was saying, but she was in so much pain she was lashing out. It wasn't surprising. What she'd been through would be enough to make even an adult struggle.

Ruth shifted closer to the girl who had sunk to her knees at the base of the Christmas tree and swiped at tears as she hung the small plaster ornament. Ruth wrapped her in her arms, and when Bethany finally allowed herself to shed tears, Ruth pulled her closer as the girl sobbed into her chest. "I know it's hard," Ruth said soothingly as she stroked her hair.

"It's not fair," Bethany choked through hard sobs. "It's just not fair."

"You're right. It's not fair," was all Ruth could say. And she meant it. She knew God had a plan for each of them, but it didn't make a little girl losing her mother any easier to bear.

As she hugged Bethany, she prayed silently for her, asking God to heal her hurting heart, and that she might come to know the love that passes all understanding, because nothing other than the healing love of God would truly help her.

CHAPTER 12

*J*onathon wasn't avoiding his family on purpose. The issues with the Christmas Eve Extravaganza had turned out to be much more complicated than simply hiring a replacement caterer. There'd also been trouble with the final inspection at the community centre. If he hadn't spent the last two days calling in every favour he'd ever garnered with the city planning board, the community centre may not have opened in time to host the party.

There was no way he could leave so many families high and dry the day before Christmas, not with so much riding on the success of the Bayside project. And it wasn't a task he felt comfortable palming off to any of his staff. It was *his* project, and he would see it through to completion.

But now he was bone tired. It was the first day in almost three that he'd been able to arrive home before midnight, and he was looking forward to seeing his kids. And if he were honest, he was also looking forward to seeing Ruth. *Strictly professional of course.* It had nothing to do with her soft, reassuring voice, or the tenderness she was showing his children. It was only curiosity that drove his desire to catch up with the new nanny. After all, what kind of boss would he be if he didn't check in with his staff, and especially the new members?

The moment he walked into the house he sensed something was different. The normal entrance lights weren't on. Instead, a warm glow emanated from a pair of holly wrapped candles on the mahogany entrance table, and lights twinkled on a Christmas tree in the far corner beside the Grant Featherston lounge chair his mother had bought recently to fill the empty space.

The tree was the formal one Larissa had always insisted be in the main entry to greet guests but since her passing had been stored in the garage.

Growing curious, he set his briefcase down and hurried to the living room, drawn by his youngest daughter's giggles and his eldest daughter's laughter. Nothing could have prepared him for the sight he walked in on.

Ruth was seated in the middle of the living room floor, surrounded by all three children dressed in holiday themed pyjamas, their attention focused wholly on her as she read to them, her face animated as she supplied the voices of the various characters.

And then his attention turned to the tree looming large over the room. It was draped with delicate tinsel and flashing lights, and from every branch hung ornaments of various shapes, sizes and colours, each holding precious memories. He felt a crack at the back of his throat.

Despite the memories invoked, the tree was a sight for his

sore eyes. It was simply dazzling. He let out a small cough, and all three children, as well as Ruth, looked up. She successfully disarmed him with her smile.

"Dad!" Molly yelled as she jumped up and ran towards him. "Look what we did today with Ruth." She flung her arms wide. "It looks like Christmas!"

Sweeping his youngest daughter in his arms, he spun her around. It didn't matter how tired he was, because her enthusiasm invigorated him. "It looks great," he said, before mouthing a thank you to Ruth who simply nodded. "It must have taken you guys all day."

"It did. Dwayne helped before he had to go home for dinner," Stuart added.

"Do you really like it, Dad?" Bethany asked.

He put Molly down and walked over to the tree, giving a good show of looking it up and down.

"Indeed, I do." Decorating for Christmas was something Larissa had always enjoyed doing with the children, but in the past four years, while he ensured the children had presents to open on Christmas morning and they enjoyed a lovely dinner with his mother and stepfather, he would be the first to admit he didn't give the holiday his all, not like he had when Larissa was alive. But now, looking at all the work his children and Ruth had put into decorating the tree and the house, he was happy they had. It looked wonderful.

The two younger children surrounded him at the tree, buzzing like busy bees showing him this ornament and that. Even Bethany was exhibiting a little enthusiasm, although she still hung back. He'd been missing this part of his children, but now, their frenetic energy filled him with joy.

Jonathan mentally admonished himself for working so much over the last few days. He'd been expending so much energy making Christmas a special time for others that he'd neglected the most important people in his world—his children. That ended now. He wouldn't return to the office until Monday morning. He should have been here, decorating the tree with the children. He shouldn't have left it to Ruth.

He glanced over at her, the twinkling lights from the tree throwing a warm glow against her tanned skin. He found himself entranced by her. She was wearing a snug fitting V-necked white top that accentuated her tan. And her curves. Not that he was looking. Loose tendrils of rich auburn hair trailed down her cheeks, giving her a youthful, innocent look. He gulped and quickly averted his gaze. Since when had little Ruthie Reynolds become so alluringly attractive?

She must have sensed his gaze on her because she pushed to her feet and brushed imaginary dirt from her capri pants while addressing the children. "All right, kids, it's getting late and I'm sure your dad is tired. Why don't we say goodnight?"

"Do we have to?" Molly pleaded.

"I think so. It's way past your bedtime, young lady." Ruth ruffled his youngest daughter's hair and smiled.

"Me and Beth too?" Stuart asked. "We should be able to stay up longer since we're older."

"It's past your bedtime too," Jonathon said, "and it looks like you've had a busy day. I'll be home all weekend so let's plan to do something fun in the morning."

"Really?" Stuart asked eagerly.

Once again, a pang of guilt hit Jonathon right in the solar plexus. Had he really been so absent that the suggestion of doing something fun together could make his son this excited? He nodded. "Really. No work for me this weekend."

Stuart hugged him so tightly he almost lost his footing. "That's cool, Dad. Can we go bike riding?"

Jonathon chuckled and hugged him back. "Maybe. We'll talk about our options in the morning."

"Okay. Can you put us to bed, then?"

"Sure. I don't see why not. Come on." He draped his arms around his two youngest children and walked with them up the stairs with Bethany following behind. Something had changed in his eldest daughter. It had to be Ruth. Already she was making a difference in his children's lives.

A SHORT WHILE LATER, after the children were tucked in bed, Ruth was heading to her rooms when John asked if she'd like to join him for a drink. Despite her resolve to keep her emotional distance, her heart began to beat faster. He was close enough for her to see the stubble on his face and the dark circles under his eyes. His white business shirt had lost its crispness and was open at the neck, revealing wisps of dark hair.

She let out a sigh. She shouldn't accept his offer, but she was helpless not to. "I'd love to. Thank you." She walked with him downstairs to the living room.

"The house looks nice," he said as he made his way to the drinks' cabinet on the side wall.

"Thanks," she replied. There was something different about

John this evening, and she wasn't sure how to respond. She was pleased he'd come in before midnight, and happier still that he wasn't upset with the decorations. Not that she would have backed down. She had a speech prepared on the importance of Christmas for the children just in case he'd decided to take her to task for decorating the house without seeking his approval. But she was glad he didn't seem to mind at all, and that he even seemed pleased.

"What would you like to drink? Wine? Soda? Coffee?"

"Can I be boring and just have water?"

"Sure. I'll join you. Sparkling or still?"

"Still is fine, thanks."

He took two long glasses from the shelf and placed several ice cubes in each before filling them with chilled water. He smiled as he handed her one. "Shall we sit?"

She nodded and headed to the couch closest to the tree. He sat opposite.

"Bethany seemed in a good mood tonight," he said.

"That's something I wanted to talk to you about. This afternoon she had a meltdown."

"Really?"

Ruth nodded. "Yes, but it was good in many ways. I think she's been bottling how she feels about everything."

He sighed heavily. The ice in his glass tinkled as he swirled the water around. "That's probably my fault."

"How do you figure that?"

He paused before he looked up and held her gaze. "Because I've been bottling mine, too."

Her heart beat a little faster. Although she knew he was

talking about his feelings for Larissa, his voice, soft and gentle, slid under her skin and seeped into her bones. That wasn't meant to happen. Not at all, but her heart was fluttering inside her chest and there was little she could do to stop it.

"I know I've buried myself in my work to avoid facing my grief, but lately I've felt a bubbling just below the surface, a build-up of ignored emotion, and I knew I'd have to face it sooner or later."

"I'm...I'm sorry if I've done or said anything that's made it worse." Her voice faltered, and for a moment, she thought it would betray her.

He gave an unexpected chuckle. "Not at all. I'm thinking that maybe God sent you to rescue us."

She blinked. She hadn't seen that coming. Had she heard correctly? *John thought God had sent her to rescue them?* Goodness. "Did...did you know Bethany's angry at Him?"

He winced. "That's probably my fault, as well." He paused. Took a slow breath. Stared at his glass. Tinkled the ice cubes. "When Larissa died, my faith was shaken, although hers never once wavered. It astounded me. She was in so much pain, yet she trusted God implicitly." He met her gaze. "I still don't understand why He didn't heal her. She was a mother with three young children." His voice caught and his eyes moistened.

"You don't have to go on," she said gently.

"It's okay. It's good to talk about it."

"Yes, I agree. Talking helps. I won't patronise you with platitudes, John. I'm sure you've had enough of those. I can't even begin to imagine the grief you've felt, but I do know that Larissa wouldn't want you wallowing in it for the rest of your life. She'd want you to appreciate every day and help your children to do the same." Goodness. Where were these words coming from? Her heart pounded.

He looked stunned. She didn't blame him. Shy little Ruthie Reynolds would never have spoken to him like that.

"I'm sorry, John. I didn't mean to be quite so blunt."

He drew a slow breath. "It's okay. My mother's been saying the same to me for years. I think the truth is that I just don't want to let go."

"Do you think you can try to start?"

He shrugged. "Maybe."

"God loves you, John. He didn't take Larissa away as a punishment. Don't let what's happened shake your faith in His unfailing love for you."

"Sometimes He feels so far away."

"You can do something about that."

He frowned. "What do you mean?"

"God hasn't changed. He hasn't moved. You have. You've taken your eyes off Him and put your focus on other things. Good things. Just not God."

He blew out a long breath and ran his hand along the side of his head. "Maybe you're right. I don't know."

"Why don't you go to church on Sunday, especially since Christmas is close and you're home this weekend? It could be good for both you and the children."

He stared at the tree as if he were thinking. Ruth sensed he was having an internal battle. She wondered how long it had been since he'd attended church with the kids. Finally, he replied, "Let me think about it."

"Sure." She smiled. God had His hand on him and the children and she needn't worry. He was the One who would do the work in their hearts, not her.

Now seemed the perfect time for her to bring up one more subject. She took a deep breath. "There's one more thing…"

He gave a small chuckle. "Yes?"

"Bethany wants to take surfing lessons." Ruth held her breath, watching his face intently for his reaction.

"Surfing lessons?"

She nodded. "Yes. Surfing lessons. She was afraid to ask you. She wouldn't tell me why she's afraid, but I promised I'd talk to you about it. You should speak with her. She loves you and craves your approval, John. Supporting her could be a way for you to reconnect." She swallowed hard. Had she overstepped the mark again?

"Surfing lessons, huh? In a million years I would never have guessed that."

"I know. It surprised me, too, but she's really keen. Will you speak with her about it?"

John's eyes sparkled with amusement. "Yes, Ruth, I'll talk with her about it."

She chuckled. "Great. Thank you." Pleased with how agreeable he was, she decided to quit while she was ahead. Setting her glass down on the side table, she stood and bid him goodnight while promising herself she'd do her best to think of Bethany, Stuart and Molly and not how the lights of the Christmas tree reflected on John's skin, or his teeth when he smiled. Nor how her heart had skittered every time their gazes met.

"Goodnight, then," she said as she headed out of the living room.

"Goodnight, Ruth," he replied with a smile that could so easily be her undoing.

CHAPTER 13

The following morning, Ruth shifted the tray laden with pastries and other delicious breakfast items that Madeline had left on the patio out of her reach, and sat back in her chair to watch John playing with the children on the lawn. True to his word, he'd stayed home instead of going to the office, and the children, especially Stuart and Molly, were having a ball with him. How much happier they'd be if only he'd spend more time with them.

"It's nice to see them laughing."

Ruth turned and smiled at John's mother, Peggy, who was walking towards her carrying a carafe of coffee and two mugs.

"I couldn't agree more. Let me help with that." Ruth pushed her chair back and stood, preparing to help the older woman.

"Nonsense. Sit down and enjoy a well-deserved break."

Ruth sat. She knew better than to argue with the stately woman.

Peggy proceeded to pour two mugs of coffee and then

handed one to Ruth. While she sipped her coffee, Peggy turned her focus to the group on the lawn. "You've been very good for them, and I don't just mean the children."

A warm blush crept up Ruth's neck and into her face. "Th… thank you." Goodness, what a way to start a conversation.

"Jonathon told me you knew each other as children."

Ruth gulped. What else had John told her? "Yes, we went to Sunday School together for a while."

"I think I remember your mother. Eleanor Reynolds? Is that right?"

Ruth nodded. "Yes, that's her."

"How is she?"

A smile grew on Ruth's face. She'd talked to her mother just a little earlier and had heard all of her news. "She's good. She and my dad are looking forward to retiring soon."

"Do they still live in St. Kilda?"

"Yes. In the same house I grew up in."

"Will you give her my regards when you next talk to her?"

"I…I will." Ruth was tempted to ask Peggy how she'd ended up marrying a billionaire when she'd come from the same impoverished background as she had but thought better of it. It would seem way too forward. However, she could ask John. She'd heard the stories of a local woman marrying a billionaire property developer, but she'd never taken much notice. It was gossip, and at age fifteen she hadn't been overly interested, although never in her wildest dreams had she thought it would have been John's mother. She'd wondered why he'd suddenly disappeared, but by that stage, Wayne Taylor had caught her attention and she'd left it at that, not putting two and two together until now.

"I hope you intend to stay, Ruth."

Ruth blinked. She hadn't expected to hear words like that from Peggy Montgomery. She'd been half expecting Molly to ask her again to stay but was grateful the little girl seemed to have forgotten her request. Now Ruth was torn. It had never been her intention to stay longer than the holiday period. In fact, she'd had a call from the bank manager just the previous day asking if she was intending to go ahead with the loan application. She'd told him yes, and she was really looking forward to moving into her own new apartment. But something was shifting inside her. In the short time she'd been here, the children, even Bethany, had endeared themselves to her, and now she wondered if perhaps staying and caring for them might be what God planned for her instead of getting her own place and another job in the city. But it was oh, so hard to consider giving up that dream. The dream she'd held for so long. It would only be a tiny apartment, but it would be hers. And it would be brand new.

But seek first the kingdom of God and His righteousness, and all these things will be added to you.

Ruth gulped as the memory verse she'd learned at Sunday School flashed through her mind. *Oh Lord, please forgive me. I do only want to do Your will. Please show me what that is.*

She turned to Peggy and sighed. "I'm not sure what my plans are yet, but I told John when I took the job that I could only commit to the holiday period."

Reaching out, Peggy tapped Ruth's wrist and looked at her over her glasses. "I think he'd want you to stay longer than that."

Ruth gulped. She hadn't missed the meaning in the older

woman's words, but it was nonsense to even entertain the idea that something could happen between her and John. He was still grieving for his wife for one thing, plus he was a billionaire property developer. She lived week to week. Although they shared the same background, their lives now were poles apart. She looked away, unable to hold the woman's gaze any longer. If she were honest, however, she could no longer deny that it was only the children who had endeared themselves to her.

She chewed her lower lip and stole a look at him on the lawn. It would be so easy to fall for him. But it would never work. Never.

Peggy continued. "When Larissa passed away, Jonathon was angry with God for not healing her and threw himself into his work. That was his way of coping. It breaks my heart to see him so lost. I pray for him daily, but until now, my prayers have been unanswered."

The heartache in Peggy's voice touched Ruth. She loved her son dearly, something Ruth could relate to. She faced the woman and smiled. "He said he might come to church tomorrow."

Tears welled in Peggy's eyes and she reached out and squeezed Ruth's hand. "That is the best news I've heard in a long time. You may just be the miracle I've been praying for."

Ruth gulped again. *Goodness.*

Since John was home, Ruth had the day off. She could have driven back to the city and visited her parents, or gone back to her apartment and started packing, but she needed time alone.

In the short time she'd been here, so much had shifted in her life.

She headed to the beach and began walking. After leaving Point Leopold, the beach grew deserted, but she didn't mind. That was what she was after. Solitude. She came to a group of rocks and sat down, allowing the wind and the waves and the fresh, salty air to wash over her. Renew her. She also prayed, and asked God for direction. *Lord, I don't know what my future holds, but I entrust You with it. Right now I'm confused and unsure. I can't allow myself to fall in love with John, but I'm afraid that if I stay, I will. But I've also grown fond of the children, and the thought of going back to the city and living alone, even in my own place, doesn't excite me anymore. Show me what You want me to do, dear Lord. I want to be obedient and do Your will.*

She walked on further until peace settled in her heart. There was something about a windswept, desolate beach that allowed God to reach into the depths of the heart. On the return journey, Ruth found herself singing worship songs and her soul soared like the seagulls hovering above the ocean.

WHEN SUNDAY MORNING CAME, Ruth wondered what John had decided about church. After her walk along the beach, she'd stayed in her room allowing him to spend the full weekend with the children. She was extremely hopeful he'd decided to come and that God had been speaking to him. And that he'd been listening.

Having spent time away from the family, she'd come to see things more objectively, and although she'd told God she was willing to do whatever He wished, she felt convinced that staying here and becoming a permanent nanny to the children was not where she belonged, despite what Peggy had said. Cosy evening chats with John and cuddles from his children would only lead to heartache. She couldn't trust herself not to fall in love, so she needed to stay firm to her original intentions and start looking for a job in the city.

But when she walked downstairs and saw him with the children, her resolve was completely shattered. He was wearing casual trousers and a pale pink polo shirt that hugged his trim body in a way that made her think thoughts she knew she oughtn't. Especially since they were about to go to church, so it seemed. *Lord, I'm so sorry. Please forgive me.*

He looked up and smiled, his warm hazel eyes reaching her, entwining her heart with their softness. "There you are! We wondered if you were coming."

Ruth swallowed. Nodded. How could she be so weak?

"Ruth, do you like my dress?" Molly gave a twirl and then grabbed Ruth's legs, looking up at her with adorable blue eyes.

Relieved by the distraction, Ruth couldn't help but smile. "It's gorgeous, Molly." She bent down and hugged the little girl. As she straightened, she met John's gaze and her stomach fizzed. No. She couldn't allow that to happen. Quickly averting her gaze, she straightened Stuart's collar. "There, that's better."

John glanced at his watch. "We'd better get going or we'll be late." He ushered everyone to the front door.

"I was planning on driving myself," Ruth said as they approached the garage.

"Come with us, Ruth," Molly pleaded, grabbing her hand.

"You may as well," John said. "We're both going to the same place."

What choice did she have? Against her better judgement, she agreed and slid onto the front seat of the luxury vehicle. Beside John. *Get a grip, Ruth. We're going to church, and this is a momentous occasion in his life. Stop acting like a twelve-year-old with a crush.*

She could tell he was nervous by the way he chattered in the car and rubbed his hands together when they climbed out. She wanted to put him at ease. It wasn't just the physical act of going to church that was happening here, but a shifting in his heart. His spirit. Would he open them both to the Lord again? Expose his innermost hurts to the God he blamed for taking his wife too early? If only he knew how much pain God Himself suffered when His children turned away from Him and chose to go their own way. He wasn't a God who was immune to pain. Not at all. He felt it as much or more than any human ever could. But that's why He understood. "Are you okay?" she asked quietly.

He looked at her and nodded. "Yes. Let's go in." As he placed his hand momentarily on the small of her back, warmth from his touch shimmied up her spine. She daren't look at him lest feelings she couldn't, or perhaps didn't want to admit, were evident on her face. Who was she kidding? She was falling for him, and falling fast.

When they entered the chapel, she nodded hello to Peggy and Mathew who had arrived before them. The older woman smiled and dabbed the corner of her eye. Ruth squeezed past them to the far end of the pew to allow the two younger children to sit beside their father. Bethany had come in last and sat beside her grandmother. Ruth couldn't shake the feeling that this was what family was supposed to feel like. Three generations worshipping together.

She drew a calming breath, and facing the front, prayed silently that God would touch hearts today. Hers included.

The service was more formal than she was used to. Instead of a band, an organ played the introduction to one of Ruth's favourite Christmas songs, 'O Holy Night'. The words gave glory and honour to God and alluded to the hope that Christ brought to the world when He humbled Himself and came to earth as a baby. As she joined in, peace filled her heart and she knew that God in His wisdom would work everything out. He was truly trustworthy and knew what He was doing. Even if she didn't.

O holy night the stars are brightly shining
It is the night of our dear Saviour's birth
Long lay the world in sin and error pining
Till He appeared and the soul felt its worth
A thrill of hope the weary world rejoices
For yonder breaks a new and glorious morn
Fall on your knees
O hear the angels' voices
O night divine
O night when Christ was born
O night divine o night
O night divine

When the service was well underway, Ruth sneaked a look down the pew and her heart warmed—the sermon seemed to have captured John's full attention. On either side of him,

Molly and Stuart were fidgeting, not unexpected since the children's programme wasn't on because of the holidays.

Ruth's gaze travelled further to Bethany. She was twirling her hair and staring at a boy three pews up on the left. A good-looking boy with sandy blond hair that he every so often flicked off his face. If Ruth could put an age to him, she guessed he was twelve or thirteen. As she glanced between the two, she recalled her own childhood when she'd sat in a church very similar to this one, her focus on John as she waited desperately for Sunday School to start so she could be near him. She knew exactly how Bethany felt.

She returned her focus to the sermon. The minister spoke well, and she prayed his Christmas message was touching John's heart.

"Jesus came to earth to bring hope to a lost people. God incarnate humbled Himself and came to earth as a human, becoming a substitute for all of humankind's sin when He died on the cross so that all who believe might have eternal life. During this festive season the focus is placed on His remarkable birth, but many miss the true significance of Christmas which can only be truly appreciated when His death and resurrection are also considered.

"The sinless Saviour of the world was born to satisfy God's justice by dying on our behalf. The sinless for the sinful. He died a painful death on the cross for each and every one of us. We shouldn't simply see Jesus as the baby in the manger, but the One who conquered death and sin, and rose again, giving us all hope for an eternity with the Father.

"Isaiah chapter 53 describes the life and death of Jesus perfectly. Let me read it to you.

Who has believed our message
and to whom has the arm of the Lord been revealed?
He grew up before him like a tender shoot,
and like a root out of dry ground.
He had no beauty or majesty to attract us to him,
nothing in his appearance that we should desire him.
He was despised and rejected by mankind,
a man of suffering, and familiar with pain.
Like one from whom people hide their faces
he was despised, and we held him in low esteem.
Surely he took up our pain
and bore our suffering,
yet we considered him punished by God,
stricken by him, and afflicted.
But he was pierced for our transgressions,
he was crushed for our iniquities;
the punishment that brought us peace was on him,
and by his wounds we are healed.
We all, like sheep, have gone astray,
each of us has turned to our own way;
and the Lord has laid on him
the iniquity of us all.
He was oppressed and afflicted,
yet he did not open his mouth;
he was led like a lamb to the slaughter,
and as a sheep before its shearers is silent,
so he did not open his mouth.
By oppression and judgment he was taken away.
Yet who of his generation protested?
For he was cut off from the land of the living;

for the transgression of my people he was punished.
He was assigned a grave with the wicked,
and with the rich in his death,
though he had done no violence,
nor was any deceit in his mouth.
Yet it was the Lord's will to crush him and cause him to suffer,
and though the Lord makes his life an offering for sin,
he will see his offspring and prolong his days,
and the will of the Lord will prosper in his hand.
After he has suffered,
he will see the light of life and be satisfied;
by his knowledge my righteous servant will justify many,
and he will bear their iniquities.
Therefore I will give him a portion among the great,
and he will divide the spoils with the strong,
because he poured out his life unto death,
and was numbered with the transgressors.
For he bore the sin of many,
and made intercession for the transgressors.

"But He didn't remain dead. Hallelujah. He rose and ascended to heaven, gaining victory over death. As believers, we have that same hope, that same confidence. Death is not the end, it's the beginning of an eternity with God.

"As Christmas day approaches, I pray that you'll reflect on *your* reason for celebrating Christmas, and that you'll join me in bowing your knee and your heart before our almighty Saviour. Let us pray."

Overwhelmed by the message of the gospel the pastor had

just presented, Ruth bowed her head in humble adoration and prayed that John, too, would be doing the same.

The pastor began, his voice quiet, humble. "Dear Heavenly Father, we come before You in awe of what You have done for us. That You would send Your only Son to earth to be a sacrifice for us is the most amazing act of love the world has ever witnessed. We thank You, Lord, for that love that has the power to transform lives. It's my prayer that today each and every person here will grasp that love with both hands and choose to live for You. In Your Son's precious name we pray. Amen."

Standing for the final hymn, Ruth glanced at John. He had an arm around Stuart and Molly and was holding them close. A lump formed in her throat. As she joined the congregation and sang 'Joy to the World', her spirit lifted further.

At the end of the carol, the organist continued to play quietly in the background while everyone greeted each other with handshakes and smiles.

Ruth caught John's gaze briefly as she gathered her purse and followed Stuart out of the pew. The nod he gave her suggested that his heart had indeed been touched, and that made her own heart swell with praise.

THE CHURCH COURTYARD had changed little in almost four years. Memories of him and Larissa chatting with their friends after the morning service threatened to overwhelm Jonathon. In fact, just being in church had threatened to do that. He needed to move on. He knew that. It was doing him no good reminiscing constantly. He was living in the past, but he needed to move forward, for his own sake and that of his children.

The service had challenged him. Especially the message. Who was he to blame God for Larissa's death when He'd given up His only Son? Jonathon couldn't imagine the pain that must have caused Him, nor the pain that Jesus endured on the cross. The sacrifice He'd made was beyond measure. He'd bowed his head and told God he was sorry. It wasn't enough, but it was a start.

He was hovering in the courtyard on his own after Stuart and Molly had disappeared with some friends from school when Mathew approached and squeezed his shoulder gently. "It's nice to have all the family at church again," he said, his face crinkling in a smile. His shaking seemed less this morning than usual.

"Yes, it is nice," Jonathon replied. He probably should never have stopped going. *Why* had he? "Would you like a coffee?"

"That would be great. Your mother's off with your new nanny, introducing her to everyone. I must say, she's good with the children, and your mother seems to enjoy her company as well."

Jonathon smiled as he caught sight of his mother introducing Ruth to a group of ladies. He couldn't help but be taken with Ruth. She was simply delightful. A breath of fresh air. And yes, she was very good with the children. "She is," he finally replied.

"Pretty, too." Mathew gave him a wink.

"Come on now, Mathew." Jonathon laughed off the comment, but he would have been blind not to have noticed that little Ruthie Reynolds had grown up so very well. She was beautiful, smart, gentle, and caring, but she was also his employee. Off limits.

"What are you two handsome gentlemen over here talking about?" His mother had left Ruth chatting with some younger women and had sidled up and given him a kiss on the cheek before looping her arm through Mathew's.

"Just saying how pretty the new nanny is, that's all." Mathew elbowed Jonathon in the ribs and let out a chuckle.

"Mathew!" Jonathon gritted his teeth. "Stop it."

"I'm only stirring, son. But don't you agree, love?" He gave his wife's hand a squeeze. "She's a good-looker."

"She is, but I don't think it's appropriate to discuss things like that here."

"Of course, you're right. But Jonathon, you'd have to be blind not to appreciate her."

Jonathon glared at his stepfather. But he wasn't really annoyed. More amused than anything. And maybe he was right. Although he wasn't looking for a new partner, if he had to choose someone, Ruth would definitely top the list. "I'll go grab that coffee, shall I?" he said.

"Good idea. Thank you, son."

LATER THAT DAY, Ruth was pleased when the children asked their father if he'd swim with them in the pool and he agreed. Although it was still technically her day off, they'd invited her as well but she declined, stating she wasn't overly fond of swimming. That wasn't quite true, although she wasn't a great fan of swimming unless the day was so hot that sliding into a cool pool held more appeal than sweltering on a sun lounge watching. But if she were honest? The real reason she'd declined was because of how uncomfortable she'd feel wearing a bathing suit in front of John. Not that her suit was inappropriate in any way. Far from it. In fact, her mother always told her she should wear something less conservative and more flattering to her slim figure, but she felt comfortable in her conservative one-piece bathing suit. Just not in front of John.

Instead of joining them, she used the time to check her emails and call her mother and David. Not surprisingly, David didn't answer, but there was an email from him. He was leaving for Broome in Western Australia the following day, and from there he was planning on travelling down the coast road to the Ningaloo Marine Park where he would spend several weeks exploring the reefs and the local area. He'd also be there for Christmas. It sounded like he was enjoying himself. He also mentioned names of several people he'd befriended, one of them a female.

Ruth sent up a prayer, asking God to look after him and not only keep him safe, but to help him make wise decisions. She had to trust that his faith would equip him to withstand the temptations that no doubt he was facing daily as he travelled. He'd assured her before leaving that he would do nothing to disappoint her and that he was aware of the challenges he would face, but he also told her that he needed to explore the world on his own so his faith could be tested away from the confines of a safe Christian home. "You've been a wonderful mother," he'd said the day before he left, "but I need to spread my wings. I want to see the country God created."

She'd felt bad when he said that. But it was true. She'd never had the money to take him places. The furthest they'd been was Adelaide and that had been years earlier for a cousin's wedding. She told him she understood and promised to pray for him daily.

When she called her mother, they chatted for almost half an hour. Her mother always wanted to know everything. Ruth was used to it, but she was reluctant to tell her too much. She spoke about the children but said little about John, although she did pass on Peggy's message. Her heart was already in turmoil. She didn't need her mother making it worse.

For the first time in their lives, her parents would be away for Christmas—they were taking a two-week cruise to celebrate their retirement. Although her mother talked about it with enthusiasm, she was sorry not to be spending Christmas with Ruth.

"It's okay, Mum. Enjoy yourselves. You and Dad deserve it."

"But I don't want you to be on your own at Christmas."

"I won't be, Mum. I've been invited to spend it here."

"With John and the children?"

Ruth groaned. "It's not like that, Mum. Don't get any ideas."

"I think you like him."

Ruth blew out a breath. *More than you would ever know.* "No, he's invited all the staff who don't have family nearby."

"I see."

"Anyway, Mum, I have to go. I think I can hear the children calling me."

"I thought it was your day off."

"It is."

"Hmmm...."

"Mum!"

"Okay, love. Take care of that heart of yours."

"I am. All right?"

"All right. Love you."

"Love you, too." Wow. Her mother was so intense.

AFTER THE CALL ENDED, she wandered down to the pool complex. The Montgomerys didn't have a normal backyard swimming pool. No, the complex, because she had to call it that, was almost twice as large as the local public pool she used to pay to take David to when he was younger. This was an Olympic-sized swimming pool, complete with slides, climbing towers, play hoses and trick fountains. It was a kid's paradise.

John was sitting on a sun lounge watching them. Despite being determined to rein in her thoughts and emotions, she was pleased he was on his own. She had an idea she wanted to run past him.

He looked up as she approached and smiled. "Hey, Ruth. Like to join me?" When he wriggled up on the sun lounge, despite her resolve, she had trouble keeping her eyes off his trim torso.

"Thanks. As long as you don't mind."

"Not at all. Let me grab you a drink." He jumped up and once again she struggled to avert her eyes. He was wearing swimming trunks that hugged his trim hips, and his body was tanned a warm honey brown despite him wearing business attire most of the time. It wouldn't surprise her if there was a swimming pool in his penthouse office, although she struggled to imagine him taking time out of his busy day to sunbathe. Or work out. But work out he must. His body was too well honed not to.

"What can I get you?"

"Lemon soda?"

"Sure. I'll be right back."

"Thanks." She smiled and tried not to watch him walk to the bar.

He returned in a matter of moments and handed her the icy cold drink. She thanked him again and took a sip. It was delicious. Just what she needed on a hot summer afternoon. She drew a breath and turned to him. "John, may I speak with you about an idea I have?"

HE LIKED that Ruth still called him John. It made him feel connected to a part of his past. He'd started going by his full birth name of Jonathon when he was at university, thinking it made him seem more mature, and very few folk called him John anymore. Ruth was one of the few. Angling his head, he smiled at her. "Absolutely. What are you thinking?"

"I was watching the children playing with their friends this morning after church, and now, watching them play in the pool, I thought how fun it would be if they could have a pool party."

"A pool party? Here?"

She nodded.

In all the years they'd lived here, not one of the previous nannies had ever suggested a pool party, but why not? It made sense. "I think that's a great idea."

"Really?" Her pretty face lit up and something inside him jolted. What was it about her that made his heart tick faster whenever she smiled at him?

"Are we having a party?" Molly appeared out of nowhere and slithered her tiny wet body onto the sun lounge beside him and looked at him with eyes that would melt the hardest of hearts.

How could he resist her? He chuckled and then replied, "Indeed we are!"

"Can I invite all my friends?"

He chuckled again and kissed the side of her wet cheek. "Sure, sweetheart."

"Can I tell the others?"

"I don't see why not."

She jumped off the lounge and into the pool and dog paddled to where the other two were lying on floats. "Hey Stuey, Bethie. We're going to have a pool party and you can invite all your friends!" Her words came out gurgled as she bobbed up and down in the water, but they must have understood enough because both their faces lit up. They turned to look at him and Ruth for confirmation.

Jonathon lifted a hand and nodded. The joy and excitement on each of his children's faces, including Bethany's, was enough to confirm that something amazing was happening in his family, and he had a sneaking suspicion it was all because of Ruth.

CHAPTER 14

"Mrs. Shields, can you come in for a moment, please?" Jonathon released the buzzer on his office phone and leaned back in his chair. Almost before he could blink, his secretary appeared at the door.

"Yes, sir?"

"I need to leave, but I just wanted to make sure everything is in hand for the Christmas Eve Extravaganza." It was less than a week away, and as far as he knew, everything was on track, but he wanted to be totally sure before he left. He'd promised the children he'd be home in time for the pool party this afternoon, but all his morning meetings had run over, and now he was scrambling to get to the car.

"Yes, sir, you have nothing to worry about. The new caterer has everything in hand and the decorator has already started. You can leave it all behind and spend time with the children. A pool party, I hear?"

"Yes, and I'm late. How did you—" He didn't remember

telling her about the party, but it never ceased to amaze him how the woman seemed to know everything, whether he told her or not.

"Never you mind how I know what I know, Mr. Montgomery. The helicopter's waiting for you. I ordered it when I knew you were running late. I hope you don't mind."

He shook his head and laughed. "No, I don't mind at all. Thank you, Mrs. Shields."

"You're more than welcome. Now, go and have a good time. All right?"

"All right." He was tempted to salute her but refrained. Instead, he popped a kiss on her cheek as he passed and told her she was the best.

"Oh, Mr. Montgomery." A blush crept up her neck. "I've never seen you quite so playful, but I think I like it."

He laughed again as he hurried out the door.

RUTH STOOD BACK and inspected her work. She and the children had spent most of the day preparing for the party and had decorated the pool area with festive leis, balloons, colourful paper lanterns and tinsel. It looked like a Christmassy tropical paradise and she was extremely pleased with the result. "What do you think, Bethany?" she asked the pre-teen who'd been excited enough about the party that she'd risen early to help.

"It looks good." She was biting her nails and Ruth was tempted to tell her to stop but decided against it. They'd come so far in their relationship in the short time she'd been there, so she didn't want to risk overstepping the mark now and alienating her. "Did everyone say they were coming?" Bethany asked casually.

Ruth hid a smirk. She knew that tone of voice and what it meant. Bethany didn't care if everyone had said yes to the invitation. She only cared about one person in particular. "Stephen Mitchell will be here," Ruth replied as she pretended to busy herself with a row of paper lanterns while eyeing Bethany's reaction from the corner of her eye. Just as she suspected, Bethany's cheeks grew pink.

"How did you know?" she asked.

"It wasn't that long ago I was your age and had a crush on a boy."

"You did? Really? What happened?"

Ruth blew out a breath. "Someday, when you're a little older, I'll tell you more, but I can tell you that he grew up to be a wonderful man."

"I wish I was older now! Can't you tell me more, anyway? Did you marry him?"

Ruth swallowed hard as she recalled her own youthful dreams. How many nights had she lain in bed and imagined her wedding to John? She'd even planned her dress down to the finest detail. A Cinderella ballgown with a huge skirt that twirled and bounced and floated. It was simply gorgeous. She sighed. She knew the longing in Bethany's young heart. Of course, reality would come all too soon and her fragile heart would be broken, just like hers had been when John started dating her best friend when they were fourteen. But for now, Bethany had her dreams, and Ruth wasn't about to burst them.

"No, I didn't. But he did marry someone very special."

"Were you sad about it?"

Ruth drew a slow breath. "I didn't know her. I just heard. But no, I wasn't sad in the end. He loved his wife very much."

"Oh. Well I guess that's all right, then."

"Yes. Anyway, we need to get this finished before everyone turns up." She smiled at Bethany and gave her a quick hug. She was amazed at how close the girl had allowed her to get in such a short amount of time and could only thank God for the change in her.

A SHORT TIME LATER, when the party was in full swing, Ruth couldn't stop glancing towards the house. John was close to an hour late. She kept assuring the children he'd be here any moment, but she couldn't help the feeling of disappointment welling inside.

Madeline was busy replenishing the bowls of chips and snacks that seemed to disappear the moment she turned her back. Peggy and Mathew were seated on comfortable chairs on a terrace above the pool where they could keep a good watch on the children in case any of them got into difficulty. Not that they could do anything other than alert Ruth if something happened, but Peggy had the eyes of an eagle, and there couldn't be a better watchman than her. All the same, with so many children in her care, Ruth felt the weight of responsibility without John there to help.

Suddenly, a whirring noise came from the north and grew louder by the second, grabbing her attention. It sounded like a helicopter. No, it couldn't be. She knew John had one but had never dreamed he'd use it to travel the short distance from Melbourne. But yes. There it was in the night sky, lights flashing as it headed for the landing zone behind the garage. She laughed at the extravagance, but at the same time, warmth flowed through her as moments later he appeared wearing an apologetic grin and a twinkle in his eye. "Sorry I'm late."

She shook her head and chuckled. "At least you arrived in style."

"It was faster than driving." He grinned and opened his arms to Molly who launched herself at him.

"Daddy! You're here! Come and swim with me."

"I need to change first, sweetheart."

"All my friends want to go in the copter. Can they?"

He smiled and kissed her wet head. "I'm not so sure about that, sweetie. Perhaps another time."

"Okay. I'll be in the pool."

"All right. Just give me a moment."

She ran off and jumped onto a slide, landing in the water with a splash.

He turned to Ruth. "So, how's the party been going? I'm really sorry I'm late. It looks like they're all having fun."

"They are. But the children were waiting for you, John. You shouldn't have been late. I was worried you wouldn't turn up." Despite relief that he'd finally arrived, she couldn't keep annoyance from her tone.

"I've done it again, haven't I? Let them down."

"You're here now, and that's all that matters. You'd better go and get changed."

"Right." He turned to walk towards the house when he stopped and stared.

Ruth followed his gaze. Bethany was sitting on a pool chair next to Stephen, laughing and smiling.

"No way," John said. "Is he—?"

"Yes, that is a boy, talking to your daughter. A boy she seems to have a little crush on." Ruth held her breath as she awaited his response.

"I'll throttle him." John started to move towards the pair.

Ruth put an arm out and held him back. "You'll do no such thing. It's perfectly healthy for her to have a crush at her age, and he's a good boy."

"How do you know?"

"I saw him at church on Sunday."

"That doesn't mean a thing." His jaw tightened. "You knew about this?"

"Calm down, John." She guided him to one of the poolside tables and motioned for him to sit. She sat opposite. She could only imagine what he was feeling. His little girl was growing up and he'd almost missed it. Discovering that she was old enough to have a crush on a boy would be a shock for him, just like it had been for her own father.

"Yes, I figured it out when we were at church, though Bethany only admitted it to me this morning."

"And you encouraged it?" His eyes enlarged.

Ruth swallowed hard. She'd overstepped the mark. Again. But she'd only done what she believed was right for the girl. "You can't stop her from having a crush, John. She's growing up, and it's better for you as her parent to know what she's doing than for her to go behind your back." She held his gaze and prayed he wouldn't fire her for her brazenness. Sometimes, like now, it was hard to remember she was only the nanny and not a parent. "Besides, I had a crush on a boy when I was her age, so I know how she feels." She didn't believe she'd just blurted that out.

"Really?"

"Yes," she replied, her heart thumping. "And you know him."

He sat up, interested. "Who was it?"

Since she'd blurted the news, there was no way she could get out of this now, but if it helped him understand his daughter better, who was she to allow her embarrassment to hold him back? Besides, it was long ago. Decades, in fact. They were at an age and point in their lives now where, surely, they could laugh about her schoolgirl crush. Still, it didn't make the admission any easier, especially when he still made her heart race.

She took a deep breath and focused her gaze on Bethany and Stephen who were still laughing together. It would be easier to tell John if she didn't look at him. "Sunday was my favourite day of the week back then, and Sunday School was my favourite time."

"Mine too. What was the teacher's name? Mrs. Chambers? Or was it Childs? Anyway, she was nice, and I remember you were her favourite."

Ruth chuckled, relaxing slightly as she met his gaze. "Funny, because I always thought you were. She always asked you to help with the rowdy boys. Do you remember how much fun the holiday parties were? Speaking of holiday parties, how is the Christmas Eve Extravaganza coming along?"

"Are you avoiding the question, Ruth?"

She winced. "Maybe a little." Her voice was shakier than she would have liked and her heart thumped. "It's not so easy to admit certain things, you know." She let out a small, nervous laugh. "It was you, John. I had a crush on you."

His brows shot up.

Just then, her phone rang. She looked down, grateful for the diversion. David's smiling face appeared on the screen. "I've got to take this, sorry. Will you be okay with the children?" She showed John the screen.

He chuckled and shook his head. "Convenient escape plan." He shooed her away with a wave of his hand.

Ruth took three deep breaths before she was calm enough to speak. She still couldn't believe she'd confessed to John that he was her crush. Goodness. What had come over her? "Hello, David," she finally answered as she headed towards the end of the pool.

CHAPTER 15

hen Ruth walked away to take the call from her son, Jonathon took a moment to digest the two pieces of news he'd just received. His daughter had a crush on a boy, and Ruth had had a crush on him when they were kids. Bethany was growing up and he'd almost missed it by being too busy with work. But he felt inadequate. How could he help her through her teenage years on his own? A girl needed a mother. Someone like Ruth. He drew a slow breath. How strange to learn she'd had a crush on him. To be honest, she'd been so quiet back then he'd hardly given her a second look. But now? She'd bloomed into an amazing woman and he'd be blind not to notice her. But could he let go of his memories and open his heart to a new love? When Larissa died, he never thought he could love again, but then, he'd not met anyone like Ruth until now.

"Dad! Are you coming in?" Molly called from the side of the pool.

"Yes, sweetheart. I still need to get changed but I'll be there in a flash."

"Good." She dove under the water and disappeared for a few seconds before reappearing several metres away, a huge grin on her face. "You'll have to find me! We're playing Marco Polo."

Marco Polo? He hadn't played that since he was a boy. "Okay. I'll be there in a tick."

He quickly headed into the changing rooms and put on his swimming trunks he kept in a locker before heading back out to find Molly. Just as he spied her, he also spied Ruth sitting on the other side of the complex deep in conversation. His heart did a small flip. She was certainly a sight for sore eyes. She looked up and for a moment their gazes met before she looked away. No doubt her confession had embarrassed her as much as it had surprised him, but there was no time to explore that further right now. His children were calling him.

The party continued for the next two hours. Jonathon couldn't believe how much energy the children had nor how much food they consumed. But he was pleased to see them having fun. Even Bethany, although it concerned him that she was spending more time with the boys instead of the girls, and one boy in particular. He forced himself not to grow anxious. Like Ruth said, it was normal for her to be interested in boys at her age.

When it was time for the guests to leave, he stood at the entrance to the complex and spoke with each of the parents. Some he knew, some he didn't. However, they all seemed to know him and thanked him profusely for inviting their kids over. He was tempted to say it was the nanny's idea, but thought better of it.

Once they'd all left, he slipped his arms around Stuart's and Molly's shoulders as they walked back to where the food tables were set. Bethany was nowhere to be seen, and that concerned him a little. He knew the boy had left. He'd made a point of introducing himself to his father, a decent man with a good sense of humour. And Ruth's words had stuck in his mind... *it's better for you as her parent to know what she's doing than for her to go behind your back.* He therefore thought it wise to meet the boy's parents. And the boy. He'd shaken hands with him and looked him in the eye. To his credit, the boy had a good handshake although his face coloured. Not a bad thing, he'd decided.

"Dad, do we have to help clean up?" Stuart asked. Jonathon gave him credit. It wasn't as much a whine as a simple question. The party was over and the kids were tuckered out.

"Tell you what," he replied, spying Ruth coming out of the kitchen entrance with a couple of empty trays in her hands. "If you and Molly help load all those trays with the leftover food and take it in to Madeline, you don't have to do any more clean-up. You can go upstairs, have your showers and get ready for bed. Deal?"

Stuart looked back towards Ruth and then at Molly. "Deal," they said in unison and ran off to grab the trays.

Jonathon noted their conspiratorial grins. They thought they were pulling one over him by agreeing, when in reality it was part of his plan to get them upstairs and into bed without argument.

"That was a smart way to get them to help," Ruth said after

the children had filled the trays and disappeared into the house, her embarrassment seemingly forgotten.

"I thought so," he said. "I may have won the battle, but I think the war will be long and arduous." He bowed deeply, doing his best impression of a weary naval admiral.

Ruth chuckled. He liked that he could make her laugh.

"I saw you talking to Bethany," she said, moving around the pavilion picking up trash and pulling down the withered paper decorations.

"Yes, I spoke with her about those surfing lessons."

"That's great," she said, her eyes beaming.

John smiled back. He knew he shouldn't feel proud of doing what should be regular fatherly duties, but he did, and he wanted Ruth to be proud of him too.

"She must be excited," she said.

"She is. It's nice to see her enthused about something again."

"I agree. I'll reach out tomorrow morning and see how we can get her registered."

"That would be great. By the way, do you know where she is?"

"She offered to help Madeline in the kitchen."

"Really?"

Ruth nodded.

"Well, I'll be."

"She's coming out of her shell, John."

"So it seems." He wondered once again how this woman had achieved so much in such a short amount of time.

"How was your phone call, by the way?" he asked a moment later.

"David's doing really well," she replied with a touch of

sadness in her voice. "He's moving on to another place soon and he doesn't know when he'll be able to call again, so he wanted to say Happy Christmas, just in case he missed me on the actual day." Her voice caught in her throat. It was obvious she missed her son.

"It must be hard to have him so far away at this time of year," he said, straightening and glancing at the house. "I'm just starting to realise how quickly my three are growing up."

"Yes, it happens in a blink. But I couldn't be prouder of David. He's a wonderful young man."

"If he's anything like his mother, I would know that to be true." He'd intended his words to be a compliment, but to his ears, they sounded like a pick-up line.

They must have confused her as well because she began wiping a table that was already clean.

An awkward silence hung between them for several minutes before the children returned to say goodnight. "I'll take them up and put them to bed," he told her after they'd each given her a hug.

She nodded and gave a tenuous smile. He needed to talk to her, tell her he was sorry for making her uncomfortable, but right now, his children needed him.

EVERYTHING WAS CLEAN AND TIDY. Madeline was preparing to go home and Bethany was about to head upstairs to take a shower. Ruth had hoped she'd also be upstairs safely ensconced in her room before John reappeared. That wasn't the case. Moments after she'd said goodbye to Madeline, she was following Bethany up the stairs and came face to face with him.

He stopped to say goodnight to Bethany and then met Ruth's gaze. Her heart thudded again. How could she have been so impetuous? Revealing her innermost secret to John had been stupid. Now her heart was exposed and everything he said or did from now on would make her wary. On edge. Like his earlier statement. Oh, how she wished she could take it all back. But now it had been said, it couldn't be unsaid. If it wasn't for the children, she'd be out of here like a flash. But she couldn't leave them. Not this close to Christmas. Somehow, she'd have to protect her heart and avoid John.

"We need to talk," he said.

She swallowed hard and nodded.

"Come and have a drink."

She grimaced but said okay. It was probably better to talk about it than allow it to be a simmering undercurrent for the remainder of her tenure. But how she wished she could turn the clock back.

"Lemon soda?" he asked when they reached the kitchen.

She nodded again. "That would be nice, thanks." Her voice was wobbly and she felt nauseous.

"Let's sit outside. It's a lovely evening," he said.

She followed him out onto the patio. He was right. She'd been so busy cleaning up after the party and chastising herself over her faux pas that she hadn't really noticed. Living in the city, she rarely looked into the night sky, but here, away from competing city lights, the stars shone like diamonds.

"We need to clear the air," he said.

"We do. I'm sorry for what I said, John. It's made our

working relationship difficult and awkward. I can leave tomorrow if you'd like."

A deep frown creased his forehead. "Don't do that. The children would never forgive me if you left. But I was going to apologise for what I said. I meant it as a compliment, nothing else."

Relief, tinged with a little disappointment, flowed through her. Part of her had wanted it to be more than that. But no. It would never work. Their worlds were too far apart. "There's no need to apologise. I took it as none other than a compliment."

"I'm glad to hear that. I didn't want you to feel uncomfortable."

She offered him a warm smile. "I don't, John. And I don't want you to feel uncomfortable, either."

"I don't."

Nether were being completely truthful, but at least they'd addressed the issue.

"I'm pleased you've been spending more time with the children. They really loved having you around this weekend. They're so much happier. Your mother, stepfather, and even Madeline have noticed."

"About that…"

Ruth angled her head. She sensed what was coming. "Yes…"

"I'll be at the office more than normal for the rest of the week, putting the final touches to the Christmas Eve Extravaganza."

"I see."

"I've already lost valuable office time by taking the whole of last weekend off, and now the pool party. Not that I've regretted any of it, but now I have full days ahead of me. It's important that the Extravaganza goes off without a hitch," he explained, a little too quickly, as if justifying himself. "Top tier city officials are planning on attending, and securing rights to future projects hinges on their approval. This event can cinch that for us. It's extremely important."

"But John, your kids need you too. They're just starting to get used to having you around more."

"I feel bad, but it can't be helped. As well as the Extravaganza, the first block of apartments is releasing this week and we still have a few issues with getting the final sign-off."

Mixed feelings surged through her. One of those apartments would be hers if her loan got approved—she should know in the next day or so. But surely John had staff to look after these finer details. She asked him.

"Yes, of course I have staff. But I like to be there to oversee."

And to be in control? She didn't say that, but it was obvious that he was still using work to hide. Perhaps he'd been hiding for so long he'd forgotten how to step back and allow others to step in.

"You said you were going to address that. It seems you haven't." Goodness. There she went again. Overstepping the mark as if she were his wife, not his employee. Words she thought, but never meant to say, kept popping out of her mouth. And the tone she'd used had been judgmental. Terse.

His face grew red and his mouth took on an unpleasant twist. "I think you should leave."

She stood there, shocked. Stunned. John had fired her. It was probably for the best, but sudden, explicable loss squeezed her heart. "I'm so sorry, John. I never should have said that. But you're right. It would be best if I leave. I'll go first thing in the morning."

JONATHON LOOKED AT RUTH, hard. He could see the determination in her eyes and heard it in her voice. Her words had stung, although he knew them to be true. But could he allow her to leave? The children would never forgive him. And he wouldn't find another suitable nanny this close to Christmas. Not one as suitable as Ruth, anyway.

"Ruth, please don't go. You're right. You're absolutely right. I *have* been hiding. I know I can't keep doing so. The children need me, but I have to take it slowly. This development has consumed me. But I believe in it passionately. I feel guilty that I have so much when others have so little, and I want to give them the best leg up in life I can offer. I love the Bayside area. It's where my heart is. This home was Larissa's dream more than mine, but now that she's gone, it's impossible to leave it."

"And neither should you, John. This is your children's home, and as long as you build memories with them, like the pool party tonight, it will be a special place for you all. I admire what you're doing in Bayside. It's a wonderful development. In fact, I'm buying one of the apartments myself."

Stunned, he stared at her. *Ruth's buying one of the Bayside apartments?* By the look on her face, he sensed she hadn't meant to blurt it out. Much like she hadn't meant to tell him she'd had a crush on him when they were young. Nor confronted him about him hiding his grief. But Ruth Taylor was nothing if not honest, and once again she was uncomfortable. But more than that was the implication of what she'd said. If she was buying one the apartments, she definitely wasn't planning on sticking around. That realisation hit him like a punch to his solar plexus, leaving him with an inexplicable feeling of emptiness. "Really? Fancy that!"

"Yes. I'm tired of renting, and when I saw the new development, I decided to put an offer in on one of the apartments."

"I'm sure you'll enjoy living there."

"I'm sure I will." She pulled her gaze from his and stared at her empty glass. "I'll stay until after the holiday period as per our original agreement, but then I'll be leaving to move into the apartment. Assuming the finance is approved."

Wow. That she needed to apply for finance for a tiny apartment when he owned the entire complex must be galling for her. He almost felt like giving it to her. A strange thought, but something inside him was changing. The truth was that he didn't want her to leave. Ever. "Okay. I appreciate that. And let's put the awkwardness behind us. For the children's sake."

When she looked up and nodded and their gazes connected and held, he had to fight the overwhelming desire to hold her.

CHAPTER 16

onathon rubbed his temples and leaned back in his chair as he stared out his office window across the bay. Christmas Eve was only two days away and everything for the big event was finally in place. So why was he still here?

Most of the staff had already left for the holiday, and even Mrs. Shields was taking a much-deserved break until the morning of the event. Yet here he was, sitting in his office, alone. Ruth had been right. He'd been using work to hide from his grief over losing Larissa for so long it had become a habit. He chose to work instead of being at home with his children. What kind of father would do that?

His thoughts returned to Sunday, when sitting at church with the children, his parents, *and Ruth*, had almost felt normal. Could he have normal again? Was it possible to move on from the numbness that had replaced his initial anger following Larissa's death and begin feeling again? Maybe... Something was stirring inside him and feelings and emotions he'd thought long dead were twisting around his heart.

Just that morning he'd had an unexpected visit from his mother. Mathew had gone into respite care for the day and she'd come into the city for a day of Christmas shopping. When she invited him to have lunch with her, he knew what was coming. A good talking to. She hadn't disappointed him. They'd gone to the restaurant on the next floor down in the Towers, and while they ate, she'd asked him why he was at the office when he didn't need to be.

"I know you're hiding yourself away, Jonathon. A mother can tell," she'd said. "You think the pain will go away if you throw yourself into your work, but hiding away isn't the solution. You won't be able to move forward until you let God heal your pain. It's God's love that helps us through the darkest times and helps us to see the strength within ourselves to keep moving forward when all seems lost. Larissa would want you to be happy again and she'd also want you to find peace with God."

She was right. After listening to the sermon on Sunday, he'd felt a softening in his heart towards God but had been trying to ignore it since. But now, sitting in his office, alone, he felt the need to get right with Him.

Spinning his chair around, he shut his computer off and headed for the door.

Twenty minutes later, he stepped out of the taxi he'd hailed outside the office and began walking slowly down Hunter Street. Terraced houses decorated with Christmas tinsel and lights looped along iron balconies stretched both ways as far as the eye could see. Children playing on the footpath looked up as he dodged around them; an old Jack Russell yapped as he paused at number thirty-one.

"Hey little fella. It's okay. I used to live here." He bent down and gave the dog a pat. The house had been looked after. The paint work was fresh and the garden well-kept. His mum would be pleased. But that wasn't why he was here. He walked on until he came to the church on the corner of Hunter and Bayview.

Taking a deep breath, he walked up the three steps and then hesitantly peered inside. It smelled a little musty and old, but it was quiet, and as he walked inside, a sense that he was entering God's presence pervaded his spirit. He took a seat and bowed his head. For a moment he was unable to speak. Or think. Tears welled in his eyes and spilled onto his cheeks. Finally, he began to pray silently, asking God to heal his heart. To take his grief and replace it with peace.

Sobs wracked his body, and then a hand touched his shoulder. Through his tears, he looked up into a kind face. The face of his Sunday School teacher. "Mrs. Cleary…"

"Yes, John. It's good to see you."

"How did you know I was here?"

"I didn't. I dropped in to do some cleaning before the Christmas service and I saw you sitting here."

"How did you know it was me?"

"I've been praying for you every day since you left the class, just like I pray for all my students, past and present. I've been watching you, John. I've seen the good you've been doing in our community, and the heart you have for the people, but I've also seen the pain you've been carrying since your wife's passing."

Fresh tears welled in his eyes. She'd been watching him? Praying for him? "Really?"

She nodded. "And I'm so glad you're here. I'd love to help you find your way back to God. Can I do that?"

He smiled. "I've already done it."

"Oh, God bless you, John. I know He has great things in store for you. You have such a compassionate heart, but just make sure you love those kiddies of yours."

How did she know? Had his mother been talking with her about him? Surely not. It didn't matter. "I will."

"Can I pray for you?"

"Okay." A lump blocked his throat.

She placed a hand gently on his shoulder and began to speak quietly, gently. "Dear Lord, thank You for bringing John back to the fold. He's been like a lost, wounded sheep these past years, but You, the Good Shepherd, never stopped seeking him, calling him. Heal the wounds of his heart, dear Lord and bless him as he seeks to live for You. Transform his life for the benefit of the Kingdom, and equip him for the journey ahead. Thank You that he's already using his good fortune to help the needy of the world rather than storing up riches for himself here on earth. And thank You for his gentle, compassionate spirit. And Lord, I do pray a special blessing on his children. May they also come to grasp how much they're loved. In our precious Saviour's name we pray. Amen."

John brushed his eyes before lifting his head. "Thank you. I've been so busy numbing my grief over losing Larissa that I shut everyone out, including God. And my children. I can sense a change in my spirit already."

"That's wonderful, John. Now go home to them. It's almost Christmas, and they need you."

He nodded his head and chuckled. "Okay. I will."

As he walked out of the church, he felt lighter, as if the strings that had held him to his grief had been snipped and he was free to feel again.

And he knew what he needed to do. Ruth had been leaving notes for him each morning with the time and location of Bethany's surf lesson. He glanced at his watch. If he left now, he could get there just in time for today's lesson.

CHAPTER 17

*R*uth put a hand to her forehead to block the sun as she watched Bethany on her board. The day after the pool party she'd contacted the instructor, and thankfully he'd had room for her and invited them to come down that afternoon for her first lesson. Now, two days later, Ruth was so proud at how well Bethany was doing. Of course, it helped that Stephen Mitchell also happened to be in the same class.

"Ruth, when is Bethie going to catch some big waves?"

Ruth looked down at Molly who was digging in the sand beside her. "One day, sweetie. She needs to learn on the small waves first."

"Okay. I'm going to build a sandcastle now. Do you want to help?"

"Sure." Ruth moved closer and grabbed a bucket, but while she scooped wet sand and helped Molly create a fortress, she also kept an eye on Stuart and the dogs who were running in and out of the waves, and also on Bethany. She'd only had three lessons but already she was showing promise. But more than that, her demeanour had continued to improve. Ruth only wished John was at home to see the change in her.

Every morning Ruth left him a note on the coffee maker, letting him know the time of each lesson. It was the one place in the house she knew he'd see it because he wouldn't leave the house without a coffee, no matter how early it was. But after their discussion the other evening, she knew she had to give him time. And space. She sensed he was working through issues and she continued to pray for him. It was all she could do. She also knew that this week he was especially under pressure, although he'd admitted he had staff who could handle things.

Despite all of that, she hoped and prayed he would make time to come to one of Bethany's lessons before they stopped for Christmas.

"Ruth! Help!"

The distant sound of Stuart yelling snapped her out of her thoughts. She quickly scanned the shoreline and saw him running towards her in tears.

"Stay here, Molly. I need to see what's wrong with your brother." She met him halfway and held him at arm's length. "What's wrong, Stuart?"

"Riley's gone. I can't find her anywhere." Sobs racked his body making his teeth chatter.

Sure enough, only one Golden Retriever bounded up behind him. The other was nowhere to be seen. "Okay, love, try to be calm. I'm sure we'll find her. Where did you see her last?"

"We...we were playing in the sand. Going in and out of the

water. You know how they love that? Then there was a crab. Riley tried to sniff it, and…and it must have pinched her nose, because she yelped and ran off." Stuart wiped at the sandy tears streaming down his cheeks. "I tried to follow her, but she disappeared over the dunes. I think she's hurt. We have to find her!"

Ruth had a solid picture of what happened. She knew Riley would most likely have simply run home, but a lost dog to a ten-year-old boy was the end of the world. She looked at her watch. There was forty minutes left on Bethany's lesson, enough time to go looking and be back to walk home together. "Okay, let's look for her. She can't be far away. I'm sure we'll find her."

Stuart's face brightened. "Okay."

"Come on, Molly, let's help your brother find Riley."

Molly stood and wiped the sand from her knees before running up to them. She put an arm around her brother. "We'll find her, Stu." Her sweet voice and the love she showed for her brother warmed Ruth's heart.

They headed off, taking turns calling for the dog. After about twenty-five minutes of exploring all the tracks leading from the beach into the scrub, there was still no sign of her. Ruth was as sure as ever that the wounded pooch had headed back up the trail to the house. It was just over a kilometre and was such a familiar walk. She'd tried calling the house several times but there was no answer. Madeline must have been somewhere out of range, perhaps in the garden, and the housekeeper would have already left. Peggy had gone into the city and Mathew was in respite care, so, other than returning to the house herself, there was no way of checking if her theory was right.

She stopped and spoke to Stuart who still looked distraught. "Stuie, I bet Riley ran home, but Bethany's lesson is finishing soon and we need to go back for her. We'll head home as soon as she's finished. Okay?"

"We can't stop looking, Ruth. We're close, I know it!" He burst into tears.

Ruth hugged him tight. "I know you're sad, buddy. But we'll find her."

"But if we go back to the beach, how will she know where we are?"

"She has a great sense of smell. She'll find us if we don't find her."

"But her nose probably isn't working because of the crab!" Stuart began to cry harder.

How could she have forgotten about the crab? "Shhh, now." Ruth pushed damp hair off his face and gave him a clean tissue from her pocket. "If not, we'll call your dad and get a proper search party going. We won't stop until we find her. But right now, we need to get back for Bethany."

Stuart's shoulders fell. "Okay." He sounded so downcast that she pulled him close and hugged him.

"It'll be okay. We'll find her." She rubbed his back. "Come on now, let's go." She released him, and putting an arm around both children's shoulders, walked with them back to the beach.

Bethany was still in the water, and Ruth breathed a small sigh of relief. At least they'd gotten back in time.

Molly broke free and ran ahead to her sandcastle, but Stuart held Rex on a tight leash while he scanned the beach for

Riley. Ruth sent up a silent prayer that she was right and that Riley was at home.

"Do you hear that?" Stuart asked, his eyes shining with hope.

Ruth strained her ears. She wasn't sure, but it could be the sound of a dog's bark coming from over the dunes. "I think so, but don't get your hopes up, Stu. It could be any dog." She silently prayed it was Riley.

"It's her. I know her bark. It's Riley." He turned and began sprinting towards the trailhead.

"Stuart. Come back," Ruth called after him.

He either didn't hear, or if he did, he didn't obey. She turned to Molly. "Stay right here, sweetie. Don't move. I'm going after Stuart." She needed to get to him before he disappeared from sight. Maybe three children and two dogs was more than she could handle.

Ruth took off after him, her feet sending sand flying as she sprinted as fast as she could. Thankfully she didn't have to go far. Before either she or Stuart reached the start of the trail, Riley broke through the brush. Stuart gave a shout of glee and threw his arms around the dog's neck. But it wasn't the dog who held Ruth's attention. It was the tall, handsome man who followed behind. *John.* She could hardly believe it. He'd come.

"Look who I found whimpering in the yard." His smile was broad as he, Riley and Stuart approached together.

Ruth smiled. "You, sir, have saved the day."

"Looks like her curiosity may have gotten the better of her," he said, pointing at the small scratches on the dog's nose.

"Crab," Ruth said, trying to stifle a chuckle while taking in the pair of khaki shorts and white polo shirt that fit him so well.

"Ahh, that explains it." He ruffled Stuart's hair. "I bet you were worried, huh?"

"I sure was, but *you* found her!" Stuart beamed at his father.

He smiled and gave his son a hug. "Now that both dogs are here, why don't you go and play while I watch Bethany for a while?"

"Okay. Let's go, guys." Stuart took off along the beach, but he was no match for the dogs who quickly overtook him, Riley's sore nose obviously forgotten.

Ruth checked her watch. "She's only got ten minutes left."

"I'm sorry I didn't get here earlier."

"You're here now. That's all that matters."

"Is that her on that wave?" He was pointing to a girl on a board riding a small wave about one hundred metres offshore.

Ruth squinted. It was sometimes difficult to tell who was who, but today Bethany was wearing a pink headband and it stood out. "Yes, that's her."

"She's a natural." Pride sounded in his voice.

Ruth glanced at him and her heart skipped a beat as he lifted a hand and waved at his daughter. Something was different about him. He seemed more relaxed and his face more alive, as if he was truly happy to be there. The broad smile that lit up Bethany's face when she saw him was enough to confirm that his presence was more than appreciated.

Whatever had happened that caused him to come, Ruth was glad he'd made the effort.

CHAPTER 18

*J*onathon paused outside Bethany's room and listened for a moment to her laughter as she video chatted with a group of her friends.

He'd just come off a check-in call regarding the Christmas Eve Extravaganza. Although he'd delegated most of the final tasks to his staff, with only one day left, he wanted, rather, needed, to make sure everything was still on schedule. Thankfully it was, and he could rest easy and enjoy being at home with his family.

Knocking softly, he pushed the door open and poked his head inside.

She looked up and smiled, although she continued chatting.

He stepped inside and kissed the top of her head.

"Ugh, Dad, come on." She groaned before making excuses to her friends for her 'weird' father, but the sound of her giggles echoed down the hallway as he left her to it. She was so different from the sullen, angry girl he'd been living with for so long. Although he was happy with the change in all his children since Ruth had come into their lives, the change in Bethany was especially welcome.

She was also spending less time on her iPad. In fact, all three children seemed to be interacting more with the world around them and each other. Something else he could probably thank Ruth for.

So much had changed around the house in the few short weeks since she'd been here and he hated to think what would happen when she left. Whenever he thought of her not being here, a heavy invisible cloud of despair descended upon him.

Moving down the stairs, another round of giggles came from Molly and Stuart in the living room. He approached quietly, not wanting to disturb them. The lights from the Christmas tree made the room homey and inviting. Wearing pyjamas and eating popcorn, the kids sat on either side of Ruth on the couch while she read to them from a large book of Christmas stories. The only thing that could have made the picture any more perfect would have been a roaring fire in the hearth.

She must have seen him slip in because she glanced up without stopping. He shook his head, urging her to go on. He settled into an armchair and listened as she continued, soon finding himself entranced not just by the story, but by the storyteller.

How different this woman was from the girl he was starting to remember more as they spent time together. His memory was of a shy but caring girl. As a woman, Ruth had gained confidence. She was bold, strong, and unafraid to voice her opinions, even to her employer. Especially to her employer. Little Ruthie Reynolds had grown into an amazing, confident, alluring woman. Was it possible he was falling for her?

"One more," Molly begged. The story was over, and he realised at some point his thoughts about Ruth had taken over and he hadn't heard the ending.

"Please, Ruth, one more!" Stuart chimed in.

"Now, now," she said, doing her best to look stern. "Tomorrow is Christmas Eve and we have a big party to go to with your father." When she lifted her gaze and met his for a fleeting moment, he couldn't deny any longer that he was drawn to her. "It's an important event," she continued, looking back at the children, "so we need to brush our teeth, say our prayers, and get a good night's rest, okay?"

Both children turned and looked at him with sweet, pleading eyes.

"Oh no, you don't." He wasn't about to allow their angelic faces to suck him in. "If Ruth says it's time for tooth brushing and prayer saying, then it's time. Off to bed for both of you."

He tried his best not to laugh as they stomped their feet and marched towards their rooms after giving him a hug and a kiss and making him promise he'd tuck them in when they were ready.

When Ruth began to follow them, he swallowed hard and called after her. He wasn't sure what he wanted to say, but the Christmas lights had played with the highlights of her hair and made her look every bit the angel he was beginning to think she was.

She stopped and turned around, her forehead creased.

Standing, he slowly approached her. Lifted his hand to

touch her cheek. A sense of urgency drove him, as if now, after opening his heart to love, the floodgates had opened and he wanted, no, *needed*, to be close to someone. But not just anyone. He wanted to be close to this woman. His heart pounded as his hand lightly brushed her skin.

"Ruth! Can you come say my prayers with me?" Molly was leaning over the railing at the top of the staircase.

Jonathon released the breath he didn't know he'd been holding and dropped his hand. What had he been thinking? If Molly hadn't interrupted them, he was sure he would have kissed Ruth. And that wasn't okay.

"I'd...I'd better go," she said, her voice fragile. Uncertain.

He coughed. "Yes, of course. I'll be up in a moment."

As she headed up the stairs, he sank into the armchair and let out a struggled breath. *What had he done?* She was his employee. His children's nanny. And he'd been about to kiss her.

CHAPTER 19

*R*uth spent Christmas Eve morning in a haze. As she sat at the kitchen island sipping her coffee while the children played in the next room, her mind kept returning to that moment with John the night before.

He'd wanted to kiss her. He had that look in his eye. His gaze had darkened, and his mouth had slightly parted as he moved closer. Had Molly not called out, he would most definitely have kissed her.

The thing was, she'd wanted him to. Despite her resolve not to allow herself to fall for him again, to let him back into her heart, she'd *wanted* him to kiss her.

"A penny for your thoughts." Madeline entered the kitchen and proceeded to pour a cup of coffee.

Ruth looked up and smiled. "Oh...good morning."

"And good morning to you. What's made you so pensive this lovely morning?" Madeline carried her coffee to the counter and slid onto a stool opposite her.

"Oh, it's nothing, really," Ruth replied, shrugging. Discussing John with Madeline wasn't something she felt comfortable doing. It wasn't that she didn't trust her, but what would she sound like? *Our boss wanted to kiss me last night, and I wanted him to.*

"Is it about Jonathon?" Madeline asked, as if reading her thoughts.

"What?" Ruth looked up, her eyes widening. How had she guessed?

"It's not exactly a secret with the way you two look at each other." Madeline sipped her coffee and grinned. "Anyone with a set of eyes can see there's chemistry between you."

Was it that obvious? Ruth felt her cheeks burn. What did the other staff members think of her? That she was after his money? The thought made her nauseous. "What can I say? I feel so embarrassed, but it's true. There *is* something between us, but it's not what you think. We knew each other as children."

"Ahh! But I think there's more to it than that."

Ruth blew out a breath. Gulped. Maybe she did need to talk about what was happening. Attempt to sort out her feelings. And Madeline was as good as any to talk with. As the longest serving employee, she knew John better than most. She looked up and met her friend's gaze. "You're right. I've been trying to fight it, but I can't. Whenever I see him, my heart takes over. I think I'm falling for him and I don't know what to do."

"Aww, sweetie." Madeline reached out and squeezed her hand. "I don't think you need to do anything. Jonathon is a good man. You're a good woman. Take it slowly and see where it goes."

"But I'm his employee. It's not right."

"Is he taking advantage of you?"

"No. He's been a perfect gentleman."

"Do you feel like he's used his position as your boss to make you do things you don't want to do?"

"No, not even close." Ruth laughed at the thought. If anything, she was the one who'd been insubordinate by challenging him and trying to make him see how his obsession with work was affecting the children.

"Then I say, go for it! Maybe this is all part of God's plan. You and Jonathon might be meant to have found each other."

Ruth closed her eyes. Could she be right? Could this possibly be God's plan? Peggy had said a similar thing. Her heart swelled with a feeling that perhaps she was right where God wanted her to be. But how could it work? Once again, stumbling blocks bombarded her mind. They lived in different worlds. He was a billionaire. She had next to nothing. She was about to buy an apartment. He lived in this mansion.

Trust Me...

Ruth gulped. *Lord, please help me. Show me what You want me to do. Let me be open to whatever You have in mind.* "It's not up to me to do anything," she said to Madeline, all of a sudden feeling a surge of confidence grow within her as she considered the possibility of what could happen between her and John, "but if John makes the first move, I won't step back. Okay?"

Madeline's smile widened in approval.

CHAPTER 20

*R*uth floated through the day, until her phone rang and she learned that her loan had been approved and that she could move into her apartment in two weeks' time. Normally the news would have made her ecstatic. For so long she'd dreamed of having her own place, but now the news left her with a hollow feeling in the pit of her stomach. The prospect of living on her own, away from the children and John, left her cold. She thanked the bank manager and tucked the news away to process later.

Right now, she needed to get the children ready for the Christmas Eve Extravaganza. She hadn't seen John since the previous evening when he'd tried to kiss her. He'd left early that morning but had left instructions of where to go when they arrived. He would meet them and spend as much time with the children as he could.

By four p.m., she and the children were dressed and ready. She called for the car John said would be waiting to take them to Melbourne. He didn't want her driving because of the holiday traffic.

When the limo pulled up in the circular drive and the chauffeur held the door open for her and the children, she felt like royalty. It seemed the kids were used to this way of travel as they proceeded to show her all the accessories and features as the limo whizzed them to the city.

The children's mouths gaped as they pulled up an hour later in front of the Bayside arena. Ruth struggled to contain her own surprise. What had been no more than a wasteland less than three weeks ago had been transformed into the biggest fairground she'd ever seen. John and his team had performed no less than a miracle.

"This is amazing!" Stuart said, his eyes wide as he took everything in.

"It is," she agreed with him. Ruth held his and Molly's hands tightly as they walked along with the crowd all heading in the same direction towards the gigantic Christmas tree that was so tall it would almost be visible from the centre of Melbourne. Bethany sauntered behind, and Ruth kept checking to make sure she was still following. Bethany had wanted to stay back and attend the Christmas Eve service at their church. Ruth knew why... Stephen would be there. Her heart went out to the girl because she knew exactly how she felt, but she was only twelve, *and* it was Christmas Eve, and she needed to be with her family.

Both Stuart and Molly wanted to look at every game, activity, jumping pillow and ride they passed. Ruth kept assuring them they'd have plenty of time to come back and go on everything they wanted. Besides, nothing was running yet. Everything would start later, after their father officially opened the evening.

At the main stage, a live nativity play, complete with donkeys, cows, sheep, shepherds, wise men on camels, and of course, baby Jesus in the manger, was in action. The Extravaganza was just as John had promised it would be with a focus on the real message of Christmas—the birth of Jesus. She found a spare spot of lawn in front of the stage, and after spreading out the blanket she'd brought, told the children to get comfy and watch the play.

During the performance, Ruth's gaze travelled to the new apartment blocks surrounding the field. Her new apartment was on the third floor of the block on the left. In two weeks' time she could move in, but the prospect of leaving the children, and John, filled her with anguish. There was no way she could pull out of the transaction now, however. In two weeks' time, the apartment would be hers.

When the performance was over, John walked onto the stage and stepped up to the microphone. He looked so at ease, and Ruth couldn't take her eyes off him. Neither could Molly, who pointed at him and proudly proclaimed that he was her daddy.

He smiled at the crowd and then began to speak confidently. Warmly. "Thank you all for coming tonight. As many of you know, the Bayside project is near and dear to my heart. I grew up in this area, and I love the spirit of community that's so evident amongst you all." The crowd quieted as he proceeded to describe the importance of community, affordable housing, and his desire to help those who needed it the most. "It's my hope that this new development will give many of you the opportunity to own your own homes for the first time. Also, the training college will provide many of you with new skills so that you can obtain employment. But most of all, my wish is that this development will enhance the sense of community you already have. You have an amazing connection with each other, and that's something money can't buy. God bless you all this Christmas. Enjoy the Extravaganza. Here's to you, Bayside! Now let's sing some Christmas carols while we wait for Santa to arrive!"

A round of applause broke out as he waved and stepped away from the microphone. As the band began playing *Hark! The Herald Angels Sing*, Ruth's pulse quickened as he headed towards them. Their gazes briefly locked before he squatted down and hugged the children.

"WELL, don't you all look festive," Jonathon said as he approached his family. Without thinking, he included Ruth as part of that grouping. Despite the size of the crowd, his gaze had been drawn to her as he'd spoken from the stage. She looked gorgeous in a red blouse and figure-hugging jeans, her auburn hair bouncing softly on her shoulders. He hadn't seen her since the previous night, but all day he hadn't been able to stop thinking about what would have happened if Molly hadn't interrupted them, and now, she seemed unaware of the captivating picture she made. He gave her a smile he hoped would put her at ease, but her face flamed before she averted her gaze. The almost kiss had changed things between them, that was for sure.

"Dad! This is a really a cool party," Stuart said while Molly wrapped her arms around him, hugging him tightly.

"I'm glad you like it, buddy." He turned his focus to his daughter. "You look very pretty, Molly. Did Ruth do your hair?"

"Yes! And she said we can go on the rides soon." Her face was animated and bright.

He ruffled her hair. "Soon, but I've got a special job lined up for you guys first."

"Really Daddy? What is it?"

He smiled at his youngest daughter's enthusiasm. "How would you like to be Santa's helpers and hand out the gifts to all the kids?"

"Like an elf?" she asked.

"No, silly," Stuart said. "Elves make the presents."

"You don't believe that, do you?" Bethany said, rolling her eyes.

"Come on, Bethie, it's just a bit of fun." He put his arm around her shoulder. "And besides, I've got another surprise for you."

She narrowed her eyes. "I hope it's got nothing to do with Santa."

"Nothing at all. Why don't you turn around?"

Frowning, she slowly turned and squealed with delight when her best friend, Marcia, stepped forward and hugged her. "Dad! How did you do this?"

He gave a half shrug and a chuckle. "I have my ways and means."

"Seriously…"

He smiled. "Ruth suggested it. She thought it might be nice

for you to have a friend here tonight. Marcia's parents were more than happy for her to come since they had an official engagement in the city they had to attend."

"Thank you so much! Both of you. This is so cool." She jumped up and down and hugged Ruth and then Jonathon.

He smiled. "You're welcome, Bethie. I'm glad you're happy."

"Can we go on the rides now?" she asked.

Jonathon chuckled. It really was wonderful to see his eldest daughter so excited. "Sorry sweetheart, they're not starting until after all the gifts are handed out."

Her shoulders fell. "Okay. You win. Can we help?"

"I never thought you'd ask. But yes, you sure can."

A short while later, as the children from the community gathered around Santa, Jonathon watched from a distance with Ruth beside him. Each neighbourhood child was given a gift, and the delight in his own children's eyes at seeing the joy in others was exactly what he'd hoped would happen when he'd planned for them to help. Their upbringing was so different to what his and Ruth's had been. It wasn't their fault, but he wanted them to appreciate that not all children were as fortunate as they were, and that it was more blessed to give than to receive.

"You should feel proud of them, John. Most kids would be upset to not be receiving gifts, but not yours. Look how happy they are simply seeing the happiness in others. You've raised wonderful children."

"Thank you. Their mother would be so proud if she could see them." He swallowed hard. It was the first time he'd thought of Larissa in days and the realisation hit him hard. He was slowly letting go, moving on. He fingered his wedding band and wondered how long it might be before he removed it. Somehow, looking at Ruth, he sensed it might be soon.

She smiled. "You never know, she might be watching them right now. But whether she is or isn't, I'm sure she'd not only be proud of the children, but of you as well." She paused, her gaze lingering on his. "This is truly a remarkable event, John. This community needs a centre like this and your passion for helping others is amazing."

Her words touched him, and he wasn't sure how to respond, so he simply said, "Thank you."

After all the gifts had been handed out, and Christmas food hampers distributed to each and every community family, the rides and activities started. For the next couple of hours, he and Ruth wandered around together trying to keep an eye on Stuart and Molly as they darted from ride to ride, activity to activity. Bethany and Marcia went off on their own, although they were to check in every half hour.

Jonathon so much wanted to hold Ruth's hand. Every now and then he reached out but at the last moment drew back. He was totally entranced by her, but this was not the time or place to publicise his feelings. Nevertheless, each time their gazes met or their hands lightly brushed, the pull was stronger.

The evening concluded with an explosive round of fireworks and a prayer by one of the local ministers. After all the planning, Jonathon couldn't have been more pleased with the way the event had gone off without a hitch. He owed his team a debt of gratitude, and now, he needed to help pack up.

He turned to Ruth and told her he needed to stay behind, but as the words rolled off his tongue, she placed a hand on his arm and looked him in the eye. "Jonathon, you have people for that. It's Christmas Eve, come home with your children. *They need you*."

It was the first time she'd called him Jonathon, and the sound of it made his heart sing.

He nodded. "You're right, let's go home."

CHAPTER 21

*J*onathon sat opposite Ruth in the limousine on the way home, flanked by Stuart and Molly who chatted almost non-stop the whole way about the rides they'd been on and the awesome fireworks at the end. Ruth remained quiet except for the occasional word with Bethany. Her friend, Marcia, had been collected by her parents, and she seemed content to also sit quietly and look out the window.

Ruth made every effort to avoid meeting Jonathon's gaze, but being so close, it was difficult. For the most part, she stared out into the darkness, her body tense. Jonathon confused her. The whole time at the Extravaganza he'd been pleasant. *Pleasant!* Apart from when their gazes had briefly met after he descended from the stage, he'd given no indication that he was interested in her at all and she was beginning to think she'd totally misread his intentions the other evening. He might have at least said something. Held her hand. Looked into her eyes.

He'd had plenty of opportunity to do *something* as they walked around together for hours. But nothing. She'd misread him and now she was going to have her heart broken. She just knew it.

Arriving home an hour later, Ruth expected Jonathon would send the children straight to bed, but instead, he suggested hot chocolate for everyone. "I won't be long. Why don't you all go into the living room while I grab the drinks?"

Ruth ushered the children into the room while Jonathon headed to the kitchen.

"Wow!" Molly ran over to the tree where a pile of presents had appeared while they'd been out.

"Dad, Santa's been here!" Stuart shouted as he joined Molly at the foot of the tree.

"Already?" Moments later, Jonathon came into the room carrying a tray with the makings of hot chocolate, including a pile of fluffy marshmallows. "Well, you know the rules. One gift tonight, the rest tomorrow."

Ruth chuckled. That was always how her Christmas Eves went with David when he was young. He would argue, plead, and barter to stay up as late as possible, and she would do her best to usher him to bed as early as possible. Usually they compromised somewhere in between with her agreeing to allow him to open one gift if he promised to go to bed, and then he could open the rest in the morning. Seemed the Montgomery family had the same rules.

He gave her a wink, and it occurred to her that he must have planned all of this.

"Okay everyone, pick one." He didn't have to tell them twice. Ruth was surprised when each of them, including

Bethany who had now joined them, pulled out a medium-sized gift. She was sure their excitement would cause them to pull the largest from the stack.

Jonathon crossed the room to the stereo system and put on some Christmas music. The scene unfolding around Ruth was cosy, familial. It would be so easy to get hurt. This wasn't her family. She needed to remember that, and soon she would be leaving.

Thirty minutes later, after the hot chocolates were finished and the children had finally grown sleepy, Ruth suggested Stuart and Bethany take themselves upstairs, brush their teeth and climb into bed. However, Molly had fallen asleep in her father's lap as he sat in his leather armchair.

It was a picture-perfect father and daughter snap. Molly's sweet mouth rimmed with chocolate. Christmas lights dancing on her hair. Ruth didn't want to disturb her, but Molly needed to sleep in her own bed. She stood and approached Jonathon. "I can take her up," she whispered, trying to avoid eye contact with him.

"No, I'll take her. It's fine." There was a gentleness in his voice, and when he looked up, their gazes momentarily met. His eyes were soft and warm, and her heart melted. He stood slowly, careful to hold Molly so she didn't wake. As he headed to the stairs, he turned and looked at Ruth. "Have a drink with me when I return?"

Her heart lurched. She hadn't misread him after all. Words no longer seemed to work for her, so she simply nodded before he carried Molly upstairs.

≈

As Jonathon walked up the stairs with Molly in his arms, her eyes fluttered and then opened. "Is it Christmas yet, Daddy?"

He chuckled. "No, sweetheart, but it soon will be. Did you have a good day today?"

"Yes. It was so much fun. Can we do it again?"

"We'll see, but right now, you need to get to bed, and when you wake up, it will be Christmas."

"Yay!" A sweet smile grew on her face, melting his heart.

When he tucked her into her bed, she reached up her arms and said, "I love you, Daddy."

He kissed her on the forehead. "And I love you, Moll. I'm sorry I haven't been around a lot, but I promise I will be from now on."

"Can you promise something else?"

"What's that, sweetheart?"

"Will you promise to make Ruth stay? I don't want her to leave."

He sucked in a breath. "I…I don't know that I can promise that, but I'll do my best."

"Thank you." Her voice trailed off and her arms slipped from his neck. Moments later, her eyes closed.

After carefully changing her into pyjamas and tucking her into bed, he tiptoed from her room and released a heavy breath. He hadn't seen that coming.

Next, he poked his head into Stuart's room. The boy was asleep, uncovered. Jonathon walked quietly over to his bed and gently placed the cover over him. "Good night, son. I love you." His voice faltered. Obviously he hadn't said those words often enough for them to feel natural.

He backtracked out of Stuart's room and headed to

Bethany's, knocking quietly as he pushed open the door. She was sitting up in bed flicking through her iPad.

"I came to say goodnight. It's getting late, Bethie. You should turn that off and get some sleep."

"I will. I was just looking at photos."

He crossed the room and sat on the edge of her bed. "Can I look?"

She shrugged. "If you want. They're of Mum."

Surprised, he'd expected them to be of her friends. "Do you look at them often?"

"All the time."

He lifted his hand and tucked some hair behind her ear. "You miss her a lot, don't you?"

She nodded, and tears welled in her eyes.

"So do I, sweetheart. I wish she was here, but she's not." He swallowed hard and bit back his own tears. "I promise to be here for you from now on. I'm so sorry I've neglected you. It was wrong of me to push you away. Will you forgive me?"

Tears rolled down her cheeks as she nodded and threw her arms around his neck and sobbed.

He held her tight and whispered that he loved her. Tears blinded his own eyes as she cried against his chest. Finally, her sobs subsided and he kissed the top of her head. "Things will be different from now on, Bethie. I promise." He tucked her into her bed, kissed her again and then turned the light off.

He paused in the hallway and fingered the ring on his left hand. It was time. It was time to move on. He'd never forget his beautiful wife, but she was gone. He was finally prepared to admit it. To face it. The rest of his life lay ahead of him, and Larissa would want him to embrace it. Enjoy it. Treasure it.

Slowly, he twisted the band and slipped it off his finger. Bringing it to his lips, he closed his eyes and kissed it, and then placed it in his pocket.

Drawing a deep breath, he cracked his knuckles, walked down the stairs and headed for the living room.

Ruth looked up as he entered, the smile on her face warm, the shine in her eyes tender.

He approached and extended his hand. When she took it, heat sizzled up his arm and flowed all the way to his heart. He helped her stand and then pulled her to him, his arms encircling her. Her soft curves molded to the contours of his body as she sank into his embrace. "Ruth..."

She raised her head. "Shhh.... don't speak."

Her silky voice enveloped him. He gazed into her eyes and caressed her face with his thumb. He ran his fingers through her hair, delighting in its softness. Slowly, he slipped his hand behind her head and pulled her face closer. First, he kissed the tip of her nose, then her eyes, and then finally, he kissed her soft mouth. Her lips were warm and sweet and triggered a desire in him he thought long dead.

Finally, reluctantly, he ended the kiss and pulled her to his chest again, wrapping his arms around her. "Shall we get that drink?" he whispered into her ear.

She nodded and stepped back, a coy expression on her face. "Lemon soda?"

"With a dash of lime?"

She smiled. "Perfect."

He walked to the cabinet and poured two drinks before rejoining her. "Shall we go outside?"

"That would be nice."

She shivered as they stood against the railing at the edge of the patio. He slipped an arm around her and hugged her. "Better?"

"Yes, thank you."

They stood in silence, gazing at the night sky. Inside, his heart beat like a drum as he exhaled a long sigh of contentment.

"The stars are gorgeous tonight, almost magical," she said.

"They are." He turned to her. "Ruth, I…I owe you an apology and an explanation."

"Jonathon, please, it's not—"

She tried to protest, but he held up a hand. "Please, Ruth, let me finish." He trailed a finger down her cheek. "You've been right about everything. Since Larissa passed, I've been hiding my grief in my work, and I've failed my kids badly. I've been a terrible father."

"Jonathon, you're an amazing dad."

"That's kind of you to say that, but we both know I'm not. That's what I'm trying to say. If it wasn't for you…" He swallowed hard. "Well, if it wasn't for you, we wouldn't be on our way to healing. You made that happen."

"You give me too much credit, but I'm so happy you've reached this point. I feel humbled you think I've played a part in it."

"You've played a huge part, Ruth. I've wasted so much time wallowing in self-pity. Larissa would be so disappointed in me. She knew how precious every moment is. She had so very little time, and yet, towards the end, when she knew the treatments weren't working, we discussed the future and what it would look like without her in it. I hadn't wanted to talk about it. I didn't want her to give up. But she wasn't giving up. I know that now. She was allowing God to take her to a better place.

"She told me to grieve for a while, but then to get on with my life. For four years I've messed everything up, but now, I'm ready to move on. I'll never forget her, and I'll always love her, but Ruth, before you came into our lives, I can't remember the last time I laughed, nor the last time I truly enjoyed myself. The last few weeks have been amazing." He smoothed his hand over her hair. "*You're* amazing."

"No, I'm not. I'm only me."

He slipped his finger under her chin and tilted her face. "Don't underestimate yourself, Ruth. You *are* amazing. I'd love to find out the full story of how quiet Ruthie Reynolds became such an alluring woman. I want to learn everything about you, if you'll let me. Please tell me you will." He couldn't deny his feelings any longer. He'd fallen head over heels in love with the children's nanny.

Relief swept through him when she chuckled and replied, "There's not much to tell, but yes. As long as you tell *me* the full story of how John Robertson became Jonathon Montgomery."

"With pleasure." His heart swelled with love as he gazed into her gorgeous eyes before he lowered his mouth and covered hers gently, savouring every moment of this wonderful Christmas miracle. The only thing missing was mistletoe.

THE FOLLOWING MORNING, Ruth woke with a smile on her face. She lifted a hand to her lips and recalled the ecstasy of being held by Jonathon as he'd kissed her in the starlight. It was a dream come true. But two things worried her. What would the children think, and what would she do about her apartment?

But then, as if on cue, she recalled a memory verse from Sunday School: *Do not be anxious about anything, but in everything by prayer and supplication with thanksgiving let your requests be made known to God. And the peace of God, which surpasses all understanding, will guard your hearts and your minds in Christ Jesus.*

She simply needed to trust God to work it out. He was in control, and since it seemed that He'd been the one to bring her and Jonathon together, He would also work these things out.

Moments later, excited squeals reached her ears and she smiled to herself. Christmas morning with children. There was nothing better. She slipped out of bed and quickly dressed. Although she was technically not on duty, she couldn't miss being a part of the Montgomery family Christmas celebrations. With his new resolve, Jonathon had promised to cook pancakes for everyone, and no doubt he was already up and cooking. And although he'd invited the other staff members to stay for Christmas, apart from her, they all had family to go to.

She quickly checked each of the children's rooms, but as expected, their beds were empty, so she headed quietly down the stairs. After Jonathon's kiss and revelation of his feelings, she suddenly felt shy facing him, but she needn't have worried. When she reached the kitchen and he looked up and smiled, all her fears and anxiety slipped away.

"Ruth! Merry Christmas! Come in and have some pancakes."

When she returned his smile, unspoken words acknowledging what had transpired between them the previous evening were spoken with their eyes. "Thank you. And Merry Christmas to you all." She held her arms out and hugged the three children one at a time.

"Merry Christmas to you, too, Ruth," Molly said, plopping herself onto Ruth's lap and putting her hands around her neck. "You never did answer my question."

Ruth swallowed hard. "What question was that, Molly?" But she already knew what it was.

"Will you stay longer than the other nannies?" As she stared at Ruth, she wore such a sweet expression that tears pricked Ruth's eyes.

Ruth hugged her and kissed the top of her head as she met Jonathon's gaze. "I think I just might do that."

CHAPTER 22

That Christmas day was the best Ruth had ever experienced. Following their pancake breakfast in the kitchen, during which time Peggy and Mathew arrived, Jonathon announced that the presents could now be opened. The children raced ahead and sat eagerly around the tree while the adults followed. Molly put a Santa hat on his head and offered to be his helper. Ruth was amazed at the gifts he'd bought the children. It seemed he knew exactly what would please each one, and she guessed that maybe he'd had help. His mother, perhaps? Or Mrs. Shields? It didn't matter. Molly was delighted with her princess castle complete with turrets and moats, Stuart loved his skateboard kit and couldn't wait to set it up, and Bethany was over the moon with her very own surfboard.

Ruth had helped the children with gifts for their dad. With Madeline's help, they'd baked his favourite Christmas treats and placed them in a basket wrapped with cellophane paper.

They'd also made their own cards and written personal notes on them. She didn't miss the tears that welled in his eyes as he read them. One by one, they joined him on the floor and wrapped their arms around him. It was the most wonderful sight.

Later, Ruth sat beside him in church. Occasionally their hands brushed and a warm tingle of anticipation flowed through her. It was too early to say anything to the children, but the hope of a future together heightened her emotions as they sang songs of praise to God in the highest. He indeed was worthy of their praise, and when Jonathon told her later about his encounter with Mrs. Cleary and how he'd recommitted his life to the Lord, she was ecstatic.

He proposed two weeks later, the day before her apartment settled and would become hers. The day before she'd planned to leave Seaforth and return to her normal life. But her life would never again be normal. How could it, when she'd fallen heads over heels in love, not only with Jonathon, but also with his children?

They'd been out on his luxury yacht enjoying a day of fishing and exploring the bay with the kids, when he came up behind her as she was enjoying the view of the setting sun. He turned her around and wrapped his arms around her waist. Longing filled his gaze and her pulse throbbed double time.

"Ruth, you're the most beautiful woman I know and I can't imagine my life without you in it. I love you with all my heart, and I want to spend the rest of it with you. Will you do me the very greatest honour and agree to be my wife?"

Tears of pleasure found their way to her eyes as she said yes. She threw her arms around his neck and kissed him with all the passion that had been latent since she was twelve and he'd been her childhood crush.

They told the children and began planning their wedding. They agreed on a short engagement, just three months. They thought it best that Ruth move into her apartment for those three months, although no one was happy about it. Instead of employing another nanny, Jonathon stayed home and looked after the children. He promoted Gareth to project manager and turned off his emails.

They agreed they'd get married in the old church, the one where they'd met years before. Where it all began. They could have gotten married anywhere in the world. Jonathon had suggested Paris, the Greek Islands, Hawaii, but Ruth was happy with St. Kilda.

They visited the church and met with the pastor. During their visit, they enquired about Mrs. Cleary. He told them she was staying in the rectory because her husband had recently died and she could no longer afford the rent on her place. An idea surfaced, and when Ruth told Jonathon, he readily agreed. She would soon have no need for her apartment. They'd been praying about what to do with it after they were married, and now they knew. They would offer it to Mrs. Cleary.

EPILOGUE

*R*uth stood still while her mother adjusted her veil and then stepped back to inspect her.

"Oh, darling, you look so gorgeous I could cry!"

"Don't do that, Mum. You'll start me off."

"Who would have thought that my little girl would end up marrying a billionaire!"

Ruth smiled at her mother. She didn't think of Jonathon as a billionaire. Not that she knew any others, but she imagined that most would not be as kind or thoughtful or generous as Jonathon. Over the past three months she'd gotten to know him so well, and what she loved most about him was the way he truly cared for others. He had a compassionate heart, and that mattered far more to her than how much money he had. Although the money was nice, she had to admit.

"It's a dream come true. I never thought it would happen, either, but it seems that God knew what He was doing when I applied for that job."

"He *always* knows what He's doing, love. Sometimes we just have to take that step of faith and trust Him."

"Well, I'm certainly glad I did."

"And so am I. Your dad and I get three extra grandchildren to spoil now. Talking of grandchildren, I can't believe that David couldn't make it. I'm not very pleased with him at the moment."

A pain squeezed Ruth's heart as she thought of her son somewhere in the jungles of Borneo. He said he'd do his best to get back but couldn't promise anything. She'd struggled to suppress her anger and disappointment at his apparent indifference. She was his mother—surely he'd make every effort to be at her wedding. But no. He hadn't arrived and time was running out. The wedding car was already waiting, and soon she'd be on her way to the church. "I'm not either, Mum, but I'm not going to let it spoil the day."

"Good girl. I'll have words with him later."

"So will I, don't worry."

"Okay, love, your dad's ready, and the girls are too. You're all going to do great."

"Thanks, Mum. I love you. Thank you for everything."

Her mum smiled and gave her a careful hug. "And I love you, sweetheart. God bless you and your new family."

"Thank you."

Her mum stepped back as her dad stepped forward and smiled at her. "Are you ready, love?"

Ruth nodded. "As ready as I'll ever be." She linked her arm in his and walked carefully outside and got into the limousine. She was wearing her dream Cinderella ballgown with a huge skirt she knew would give her trouble getting in and out of the car, but somehow she managed.

She waved to her mum, and then to Peggy, Bethany and Molly as they drove past in the other car.

Several minutes later, the limousine pulled up in front of the church. Her heart beat in her throat as she carefully got out and smiled at the waiting photographers. Jonathon had warned her that the media would most likely be in attendance, so she'd been expecting them, but one photographer in particular caught her attention. No, it couldn't be... but it was. Standing amidst the group, head and shoulders above the rest, with a broad grin on his face, was her son. *David.* Leaving her dad's side, she pushed through the crowd and hugged him. "David! You made it."

"There's no way I could miss your wedding!" He winked and she was tempted to slap him on the cheek. Playfully, of course. Instead, she just studied him. His skin was darker, tanned. He'd also grown taller. So tall, in fact, she had to rise onto her tippy toes to hug him.

"I'm so glad you made it." Her heart swelled with gratitude.

"You'd better go in, because I think someone's waiting for you."

She chuckled. "Oh yes. I guess I should. We'll catch up later, okay?"

"Okay."

As Ruth rejoined her father, David offered his arm to his grandmother while Peggy stood with Molly and Bethany and straightened their dresses. They'd wanted the children involved in the wedding party, and the girls were excited to be

Ruth's flower girl and bridesmaid. Stuart was Jonathon's best man.

The organ sounded from inside the church, and Ruth knew it was time. She nodded to Peggy who positioned the girls in front of her before walking into the chapel to join Mathew. Molly turned and waited for Ruth to give her the nod. They'd practiced this several times over the previous days and Molly had done so well, but now that it was the real thing, Ruth expected her to be anxious. Her face, however, was bright and filled with excitement. She was going to do a great job. Ruth smiled at her and gave her the nod, and then Molly set off, walking slowly in time with the music just as they'd practiced. Ruth knew she'd be counting her steps as she walked down the aisle, dropping silk rose petals along the way.

She then gave Bethany the nod, and she too entered the chapel. Ruth was thrilled with the change in the girl. No longer a sullen pre-teen, she was now a sweet thirteen year-old, who, while she still had moments, was generally friendly and help-ful. Most important of all, she'd told Ruth she was happy that she was marrying her dad and that once again she would have a mother. Ruth had hugged her so hard Bethany had to ask her to let go. Ruth could never replace Larissa—she didn't want to, but she could love Larissa's children as if they were her own, and that's what she intended to do.

Now it was her turn. She looked at her father and grinned before they set off.

A LUMP GREW in Jonathon's throat as Molly walked towards

him sprinkling pale pink rose petals from her little basket. She looked so sweet and happy it made his heart sing. He smiled at her and she smiled back, her two missing front teeth making her look even cuter, if that were possible.

And then there was Bethany, his beautiful teenage daughter who looked so grown up and so much like Larissa it hurt. But he was okay with that. Larissa would always have a place in his heart, but his future lay with Ruth. He smiled proudly at Bethany, but then his gaze fixed on his bride, who stole his breath away. She was exquisite, beautiful like a princess.

She approached slowly on her father's arm, and when they reached the front, Jonathon smiled and offered his. Her father kissed her and then handed her to Jonathon. He covered her hand with his own, squeezing it, conveying his love.

They faced the front and the service began. They'd chosen a traditional service, and as the minister began with "Dearly beloved, we are gathered here today…" Jonathon couldn't be more grateful that God had been gracious to him and given him a second chance at love.

Finally, when it came time to exchange rings, he turned to Stuart and winked. His son had been so anxious he'd lose the rings, or worse, drop them in front of everybody, but he handled them perfectly and even wore a grin on his face as he passed the first ring to Jonathon.

Jonathon took Ruth's hand and looked deep into her eyes as he spoke the words he'd memorised. "Ruth, I give you this ring as a symbol of our vows, and with all that I am, and all that I have, I honour you. In the name of the Father, and of the Son, and of the Holy Spirit. With this ring, I thee wed." He slipped it onto her finger and smiled.

She did the same and slid the band onto his finger, and when the minister pronounced them man and wife and told him he could kiss his bride, he was the happiest man alive.

Jonathon's kiss left her mouth burning with fire. Over the months they'd been courting, she'd discovered her Prince Charming was a passionate man, but she'd asked him, *pleaded* with him, not to kiss her like that in front of everyone, and especially the children. He hadn't listened, but now, she didn't care what everyone thought. They loved each other, and if the entire world knew, she was fine. When he released her, everyone clapped and cheered. She laughed at his grin, the largest she'd ever seen, and then hugged him again before they headed down the aisle to greet their family and friends.

Mrs. Cleary was amongst them, and after spending time with their families, they paused to speak with the elderly woman who had been partly responsible for their union. She patted Jonathon's hand after he hugged her and told him how grateful she was to be part of their journey. "God has good things in store for both of you, I just know it," she said.

Ruth looked up at her husband and they shared a smile. Their future was just beginning, and she couldn't wait to see what God had in mind for them.

Many waters cannot quench love; rivers cannot wash it away. If one were to give all the wealth of his house for love, it would be utterly scorned. Song of Solomon 8:7

NOTE FROM THE AUTHOR

I HOPE you enjoyed Jonathon and Ruth's love story as much as I enjoyed writing it. This is the last book in this series (for now), but if you missed the first three books, you check them out here: http://www.julietteduncan.com/linkspage/649684

To make sure you don't miss any of my new releases, why not join my Readers' list if you haven't already done so? Sign up here:http://www.julietteduncan.com/linkspage/244397 **You'll also receive a free thank-you copy of "Hank and Sarah - A Love Story"**, a clean love story with God at the center.

Enjoyed "Her Compassionate Billionaire"? You can make a big difference. Help other people find this book by writing a review and telling them why you liked it. Honest reviews of my books help bring them to the attention of other readers just like yourself, and I'd be very grateful if you could spare just five minutes to leave a review (it can be as short as you like) on the book's Amazon page.

While you're waiting for my next book, enjoy a chapter from "Because We Loved" I think you'll enjoy it!

Blessings,

Juliette

Prologue

Lt Cl Westaway scanned the horizon, crouching low behind the scrubby hill. Creeping forward, he motioned with his hand for his men to follow. They needed the element of surprise. They'd spent days tracking this band of mujahideen, aiming to intercept them before they carried out their plans to cause more carnage in Kabul. These were dangerous and desperate men.

Callum blinked as a bead of sweat rolled down his forehead and onto his eyelashes. It was so hot, and the air, thick with dust, was almost tangible. A few metres away, flies buzzed nosily as they fed off a long dead goat.

He hated this place. Still, a few more days and it would be over. This was his last mission before a well-deserved leave. So far, things had gone according to plan, and none of his men had been lost, though one had been flown home wounded. Enough to put him out of active service for a while, but nothing fatal.

In fact, Callum had been thinking all morning that things had gone almost too well. He'd learned to take nothing for granted.

He breathed in slowly, a sudden sense of foreboding coming over him. Years in the field had honed his instincts, and he turned his head sharply to the right before he saw the figure running towards his men from seemingly nowhere, shouting a language he didn't speak, but whose words he recognised in their intent. The man's gun was raised in a fluid movement as he shouted commands to his men who followed.

It was too late. Callum's body lifted off the ground as a deafening explosion rang in his ears. As he dropped and rolled, his last image before he lost consciousness was Lt Jeff Gibbons a few yards away, staring at him with eyes that would never see again...

CALLUM WOKE WITH A GASP, his heart pounding inside his chest, his eyes wide in the darkened room.

It was a dream. Just a dream. I'm not there anymore.

Panting, he sat up and swung his legs over the side of the bed, deliberately slowing and lengthening his breath. There was no need to panic. He was safe.

As he thought it, his insides twisted with shame. Since when did Lt Cl Westaway worry about being safe? While far from reckless—recklessness had no place in the field—he had a reputation for both bravery and stoicism in the face of conflict. Never in all his years of active duty had he felt the need to reassure himself he was 'safe'.

He hadn't had these dreams until recently, since returning to his base at Salford after an active tour in the Middle East. After years in the field and a distinguished and decorated career, he'd succumbed to the lure of the desk job.

Well, sort of. He was due to start his new job the following day, training new recruits at Salford Barracks, and while he was satisfied that he'd made the right decision, he was conflicted about it. An old adage of his father's 'those who can, do; those who can't, teach' kept coming back to him. It was nonsense, of course. Callum had proved himself in the field enough times. At thirty-eight, it was time to take a step back, and Salford was delighted to have him as a Senior Trainer, believing he would be an ideal model for eager new recruits. He just hoped he could live up to their expectations. He'd had little teaching experience and if he was honest with himself, he was anxious about the day ahead, probably the reason for having the dreams. Nerves.

He padded across the room in his bare feet and downstairs to the kitchen. The three-bedroom town house he lived in, courtesy of the Defence Force, was lovely but often felt too big for him alone. He had plans to turn the spare bedrooms into a study and a gym but hadn't made a start on them yet. Maybe he wasn't ready to resign himself to a life alone, although he couldn't fathom anything else.

He'd been single since he and Danielle had divorced years earlier. Childhood sweethearts, it had never occurred to him they wouldn't have children and stay together forever. But after only three years of marriage, she'd announced she was leaving, that being an army wife wasn't for her, particularly after her friend's husband had been killed in active duty. He'd been in shock for weeks, not believing it was true, expecting her to change her mind. He waited for the reconciliation letter that never came and resigned himself to the situation by the time the divorce papers arrived. It had been an amicable enough end, and he tried not to begrudge the fact that the last he'd heard of her, she was happily married with a baby on the way. Danielle deserved to be happy. He'd settled for busy and successful.

Any dream of a family to return to after a gruelling tour was put away in a box to gather dust. Only recently, since retiring from active duty, had he understood how lonely he really was. He'd lost too many good friends in the field to be keen to make new ones, and his parents lived miles away in Frankston. His father, a retired Colonel, had frowned on his decision to take the post at Salford.

Pushing thoughts of his overbearing father from his mind, he turned the kettle on. It was never too early in the morning for coffee. He set his focus on the day ahead, hoping it wouldn't bring with it too many surprises.

Maybe tomorrow night, he could sleep uninterrupted.

Chapter 1

SALFORD ARMY BASE, VICTORIA, AUSTRALIA

Callum stood at ease, listening to Colonel Jarrop run through his first day and what to expect. He tried to hide the fact that he was so tired. The man's monotonous voice was making him feel like going back to bed to catch up on missed sleep. After the nightmare, he'd stayed awake, and sitting on his balcony, had watched the sun come up. He'd seen the sun rise in many places during his army career, but had never paused long enough to take it in. Appreciate it. That morning, he'd witnessed the beauty of a summer sunrise in a clear sky and felt lucky to be alive.

So many weren't.

The pang of survivor's guilt had followed immediately

after, spoiling his reverie. Often, his recent nightmares replayed scenes of friends and fellow soldiers dying in the field. Last night it had been Jeff Gibbons, a man who'd served under him in Afghanistan three years earlier. A pleasant guy, he was devoted to his wife and kids and talked about them constantly. Callum had still been a little raw over Danielle at that point and had tried not to feel envious of Jeff's fortune.

He'd thought of the family Gibbons had left behind a few times over the years and wondered how they were doing. He'd met his wife—Fleur, he thought her name was, it sounded like a flower—at the funeral. Even with her face twisted in grief, Callum had noticed her gentle but overwhelming beauty. He'd given her his condolences, but she'd looked through him, staring into a past she'd lost. Or perhaps a future she no longer recognised.

Seeing the Colonel staring at him quizzically, Callum pushed away his morbid thoughts. *What is wrong with me lately?* "Sorry sir, I didn't catch that."

The Colonel smiled genially. "I was just pointing out, West-away, after all of your experience in the field, dealing with a few new recruits should be child's play."

"I hope so, sir."

The Colonel rubbed his neck. "There's one recruit you may need to watch out for. Billy Cassidy. He's nineteen, I believe. He was on a fast track to prison until he decided to join the army and 'turn his life around.' A noble sentiment, but looking at his record, the boy's trouble."

Callum raised a brow. "But we've given him a chance?"

The Colonel nodded. "He shows promise. Passed all the entry tests with flying colours. Sometimes these boys are the ones who surpass all expectations and fly up the ranks. I guess because we give them a home and a purpose."

Callum smiled wryly. He could understand that. Despite his recent struggles, the army had been his home and purpose his entire adult life. "I'll keep an eye out for him. A few weeks of basic training will soon show what he's made of."

The Colonel looked pleased. "We're glad to have you, Westaway. Good luck."

Callum stood to attention, saluted and left the room. It was time to meet the recruits. His first class with them was Military History. He had them for Parade Training as well. At least he wasn't teaching PT. That would have annoyed his father.

THE MILITARY HISTORY class rapidly turned into what felt like his own biography as the recruits peppered him with questions after the lecture. Rather than asking him to tell them more about the history of the conflicts in the Middle East or the early days of the army, all they wanted to know about was Lt Cl Westaway.

"How many medals have you got?"

"How many tours have you been on?"

Callum laughed and answered their questions good-naturedly. While he knew it was important he retain his authority, he also knew their time at camp would be better supported by officers who seemed human, not just unapproachable seniors.

He was surprised by how much he was actually enjoying himself so far. Teaching seemed to suit him.

Billy Cassidy raised his hand. "I've got a question, sir."

Callum nodded at him to continue. Contrary to the Colonel's warnings, Billy had been no trouble whatsoever. In fact, he seemed happy to be there and eager to learn. Apparently he'd excelled in PT. Looking at his lean but wiry frame, Callum wasn't surprised.

"Have you seen a lot of death?" the youth asked.

Callum blinked. Was this lad somehow reading his mind? Were his night terrors on show for all to see? Clearing his throat, he answered more brusquely than he'd intended, "Of course, Cassidy. In war, people die."

There were a few nervous titters, but most of the recruits went quiet and looked at him intently. How many of them grasped the realities of what could lie before them? It was one thing to know something was going to happen and quite another to be in the middle of it. Remembering his own basic training, Callum reflected that none of the training officers had ever openly spoken about the inevitable dangers they faced, not in any concrete way. His first active tour in East Timor had been a baptism by fire. He swore to himself he'd do his best to equip these recruits with the resilience they would need.

Billy just looked thoughtful at Callum's reply. He opened his mouth to say something else, but hesitated. Callum sighed, suddenly feeling a wave of exhaustion again. "Spit it out, Cassidy."

"I just wondered, sir...maybe it's a silly question...but is it worth it? Being in the army? Is it worth all the death?"

Callum stared at him. The boy's words were like a punch to the gut. It was a question he had no answer for. He looked around the room, his gaze settling briefly on every recruit before he spoke again. "That's something you'll have to answer for yourselves. I'll ask you in a few years." *If you're alive*, he thought before dismissing them.

THE REST of the day passed uneventfully. Parade Training was frustrating, and he tried to recall how it had been when he was a fresh recruit, green around the ears and knowing far less than he thought he did. Surely, though, he'd been able to march in a straight line.

After his duties finished, Callum went home to change into gym clothes. He'd pushed through his earlier tiredness with the help of a few too many coffees and now felt unpleasantly restless and jittery. If he tried to sleep while feeling like this, he was sure to have another nightmare. A good workout and hot shower would hopefully balance out both body and brain.

It had been a good first day, he reflected as he drove to the gym. Far from feeling like he had 'downgraded', he felt privileged to teach the latest cohort and pleased to discover he had an aptitude for something other than being a soldier. Even Parade Training had given him a sense of fulfilment when after two hours of drill, a basic formation—with everyone facing in the same direction—had been managed. Apart from Billy Cassidy's question, he'd remained in the moment all day, thoughts of his recent past behind him. Maybe this was what he needed.

He parked outside the gym in downtown Salford and got out of his car. A woman had left the building and was walking in his direction. Slim and toned, with honey blonde hair pulled back in a ponytail, something about her was familiar.

She frowned as she approached, as if she also sensed familiarity. When he saw her soft, blue eyes that were as clear as the sky above, and her cute, upturned nose, he felt a jolt of recognition. *Fleur Gibbons. Jeff's widow.*

He hesitated. Should he say hello, or would she find it intrusive? He needn't have worried. She gave him a shy smile. "Lieutenant...Westaway?"

"Lieutenant Colonel," he said with a smile, "or just Callum is fine. You're Fleur?"

"Yes." A shadow crossed her face. "I met you at Jeff's funeral. I remember your name—he always spoke highly of you when he was home on leave."

Callum wasn't sure whether he felt pleased or sad. Jeff had only been with his squadron a few months; they hadn't been close. Still, he'd liked the man and often thought in different circumstances they might have met for a drink. "Jeff was a good man."

Fleur bit her lip, looking away. "Yes," she said quietly. "He was."

There was a pause before Callum cleared his throat, feeling awkward at not knowing what to say in this situation. "So...how have you been?"

She met his gaze again. Her eyes were clear and he immediately felt she was someone to be trusted. Even at the funeral he'd noticed she had a certain poise about her. She gave another small smile. "Good. It's taken a while to get to this point, but we did." She fingered a small silver cross around her neck as she spoke.

"It must have been hard," he said with compassion.

"It was. There were days when I felt the pain of loss would

never get better. But it got easier with time. That's what they say, don't they? Time's a healer." She glanced down and tucked some hair behind her ear. "It feels like nonsense at the beginning, a thing people say because they don't know what else to say, but then you wake up one morning and realise it's a little easier to breathe."

She looked taken aback at how much she'd revealed and gave a breathy, embarrassed laugh. "Sorry, I don't know where all that came from."

Callum shook his head quickly. He'd been completely caught up in her words. "Not at all. I'm glad I saw you. I've often wondered how you were doing. Jeff talked about you and the children all the time—nearly drove the rest of us mad."

She let out a small laugh and he couldn't help noticing how her face lit up. "That's so nice to hear," she said before glancing at her wristwatch. "I wish we had longer to chat. It's so nice to talk to someone about Jeff after all these years. I don't see anyone from the army anymore, but I never was one to mingle with the wives." She frowned as if realising something. "Are you on leave?"

"Not quite. I've taken a break from active service. I'm based at Salford Barracks, overseeing the training of the new recruits." He felt embarrassed as he said it, so was gratified when she looked impressed.

"That's fantastic. I bet you're brilliant at it."

Callum was surprised to feel himself flush. "Well, the jury's out on that one; it was only my first day today. I usually work out first thing in the morning, but I guess it will have to be evenings from now on." He motioned towards the gym. "Are you here after work too?" He tried to remember if Jeff had spoken about Fleur having a career.

She grinned. "This is my work. I'm a gym instructor. Yoga, Pilates and CrossFit. Sometimes Aqua Aerobics, too."

"Wow. That's great. You must enjoy it."

"I love it," she said with a simple honesty he found appealing. As much as he'd been driven to get ahead in his army career, he didn't think he could ever have said those words with the obvious contentment she did.

"I'd just finished my training when Jeff died," she continued, "so working has been a real help. Gave me something outside to focus on. That and my faith." Her hand went subconsciously back to the cross around her neck.

Callum felt a pang of something that was close to envy. He'd never really understood faith, though he'd been taken to church services and attended Sunday School as a kid. That had been his father, keeping up appearances, rather than through any real commitment or belief. As far as Callum knew, his parents now only went to church at Christmas and Easter.

"I don't know much about that," he admitted, wishing suddenly he'd paid more attention in Sunday School. He realised he wanted to impress Fleur, but wasn't sure why. Something about her drew him, and it wasn't just the fact that she was extremely attractive. Was it a sense of guilt about Jeff that made him feel almost protective towards her? Although the explosion hadn't been his fault, he always retained a sense of responsibility for the men he'd lost. Losing men was something he'd never been able to get used to.

For an instant, wistfulness stole into her expression. "That's a pity." There was another silence before she smiled apologetically. "It was lovely seeing you, Lieutenant...Callum, but please excuse me. I've got to get back for the kids."

Callum didn't know if he imagined the expectant note in her words, but found himself asking, "Would you like to go for lunch sometime? You said it was nice to talk to someone from...back then. And, well, I don't really know anyone here off base."

It seemed an age before she answered, and Callum thought he'd misread her completely and was starting to wish the ground would swallow him up, when she nodded and gave that shy smile again. "That would be nice. Here," she swung her gym bag off her shoulder and reached into it, "here's my card."

"Thank you very much," he said, and then chastised himself for being so formal. He took the card and tucked it into the pocket of his shorts.

"Right, well. See you." She gave him one last smile before turning and heading down the road.

"Bye." He lifted his hand and watched her go, feeling bemused at their encounter. Such a coincidence that he'd bumped into her the day after dreaming about Jeff.

That was why he felt drawn to her. And it'd be nice to have at least an acquaintance here who wasn't from the base. Yes, that was it.

The fact that she was extremely attractive and made him feel like a nervous schoolboy had nothing to do with it at all.

Transformed by Love Christian Romance Series

Book 1 - *Because We Loved*

A decorated Lieutenant Colonel plagued with guilt. A captivating widow whose husband was killed under his watch…

Book 2 - *Because We Forgave*

A fallen TV personality hiding from his failures. An ex-wife and family facing their fears…

Book 3 - *Because We Dreamed*

When dreams are shattered, can hope be restored?

A Time for Everything Series

A Time For Everything Series is a mature-age contemporary Christian romance series set in Sydney, Australia and Texas, USA. If you like real-life characters, faith-filled families, and friendships that become something more, then you'll love these inspirational second-chance romances.

The True Love Series

Set in Australia, what starts out as simple love story grows into a family saga, including a dad battling bouts of depression and guilt, an ex-wife with issues of her own, and a young step-mum trying to mother a teenager who's confused and hurting. Through it all, a love story is woven. A love story between a caring God and His precious children as He gently draws them to Himself and walks with them through the trials and joys of life.

"A beautiful Christian story. I enjoyed all of the books in this series. They all brought out Christian concepts of faith in action."

"Wonderful set of books. Weaving the books from story to story. Family living, God, & learning to trust Him with all their hearts."

The Precious Love Series

The Precious Love Series continues the story of Ben, Tessa and

Jayden from the The True Love Series, although each book can be read on its own. All of the books in this series will warm your heart and draw you closer to the God who loves and cherishes you without condition.

"I loved all the books by Juliette, but those about Jaydon and Angie's stories are my favorites...can't wait for the next one..."

"Juliette Duncan has earned my highest respect as a Christian romance writer. She continues to write such touching stories about real life and the tragedies, turmoils, and joys that happen while we are living. The words that she uses to write about her characters relationships with God can only come from someone that has had a very close & special with her Lord and Savior herself. I have read all of her books and if you are a reader of Christian fiction books I would highly recommend her books." Vicki

The Shadows Series

An inspirational romance, a story of passion and love, and of God's inexplicable desire to free people from pasts that haunt them so they can live a life full of His peace, love and forgiveness, regardless of the circumstances. Book 1, *"Lingering Shadows"* is set in England, and follows the story of Lizzy, a headstrong, impulsive young lady from a privileged background, and Daniel, a roguish Irishman who sweeps her off her feet. But can Lizzy leave the shadows of her past behind and give Daniel the love he deserves, and will Daniel find freedom and release in God?

Hank and Sarah - A Love Story, *the Prequel to "The Madeleine Richards Series" is a FREE thank you gift for joining my mailing list. You'll also be the first to hear about my next books and get exclusive sneak previews. Get your free copy at www.julietteduncan.com/subscribe*

The Madeleine Richards Series

Although the 3 book series is intended mainly for pre-teen/ Middle Grade girls, it's been read and enjoyed by people of all ages.

"Juliette has a fabulous way of bringing her characters to life. Maddy is at typical teenager with authentic views and actions that truly make it feel like you are feeling her pain and angst. You want to enter into her situation and make everything better. Mom and soon to be dad respond to her with love and gentle persuasion while maintaining their faith and trust in Jesus, whom they know, will give them wisdom as they continue on their lives journey. Appropriate for teenage readers but any age can enjoy." Amazon Reader

The Potter's House Books...stories of hope, redemption, and second chances. Find out more here:

http://pottershousebooks.com/our-books/

The Homecoming

Kayla McCormack is a famous pop-star, but her life is a mess. Dane

Carmichael has a disability, but he has a heart for God. He had a crush on her at school, but she doesn't remember him. His simple faith and life fascinate her, but can she surrender her life of fame and fortune to find true love?

Unchained

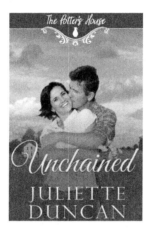

Imprisoned by greed – redeemed by love

Sally Richardson has it all. A devout, hard-working, well-respected husband, two great kids, a beautiful home, wonderful friends. Her life is perfect. Until it isn't.

When Brad Richardson, accountant, business owner, and respected church member, is sentenced to five years in jail, Sally is shell-shocked. How had she not known about her husband's fraudulent activity? And how, as an upstanding member of their tight-knit community, did he ever think he'd get away with it? He's defrauded clients, friends, and fellow church members. She doubts she can ever trust him again.

Locked up with murderers and armed robbers, Brad knows that the only way to survive his incarceration is to seek God with all his heart - something he should have done years ago. But how does he convince his family that his remorse is genuine? Will they ever forgive him?

He's failed them. But most of all, he's failed God. His poor decisions have ruined this once perfect family.

They've lost everything they once held dear. Will they lose each other as well?

Blessings of Love

She's going on mission to help others. He's going to win her heart.

Skye Matthews, bright, bubbly and a committed social work major, is the pastor's daughter. She's in love with Scott Anderson, the most eligible bachelor, not just at church, but in the entire town.

Scott lavishes her with flowers and jewellery and treats her like a lady, and Skye has no doubt that life with him would be amazing. And yet, sometimes, she can't help but feel he isn't committed enough. Not to her, but to God.

She knows how important Scott's work is to him, but she has a niggling feeling that he isn't prioritising his faith, and that concerns her. If only he'd join her on the mission trip to Burkina Faso...

Scott Anderson, a smart, handsome civil engineering graduate, has just received the promotion he's been working for for months. At age twenty-four, he's the youngest employee to ever hold a position of this calibre, and he's pumped.

Scott has been dating Skye long enough to know that she's 'the one', but just when he's about to propose, she asks him to go on mission with her. His plans of marrying her are thrown to the wind.

Can he jeopardise his career to go somewhere he's never heard of, to work amongst people he'd normally ignore?

If it's the only way to get a ring on Skye's finger, he might just risk it...

And can Skye's faith last the distance when she's confronted with a truth she never expected?

Stand Alone Christian Romantic Suspense

Leave Before He Kills You

When his face grew angry, I knew he could murder…

That face drove me and my three young daughters to flee across Australia.

I doubted he'd ever touch the girls, but if I wanted to live and see them grow, I had to do something.

The plan my friend had proposed was daring and bold, but it also gave me hope.

My heart thumped. What if he followed?

Radical, honest and real, this Christian romantic suspense is one woman's journey to freedom you won't put down…get your copy and read it now.

ABOUT THE AUTHOR

Juliette Duncan is a Christian fiction author, passionate about writing stories that will touch her readers' hearts and make a difference in their lives. Although a trained school teacher, Juliette spent many years working alongside her husband in their own business, but is now relishing the opportunity to follow her passion for writing stories she herself would love to read. Based in Brisbane, Australia, Juliette and her husband have five adult children, eight grandchildren, and an elderly long haired dachshund. Apart from writing, Juliette loves exploring the great world we live in, and has travelled extensively, both within Australia and overseas. She also enjoys social dancing and eating out.

Connect with Juliette:

Email: juliette@julietteduncan.com

Website: www.julietteduncan.com

Facebook: www.facebook.com/JulietteDuncanAuthor

Twitter: https://twitter.com/Juliette_Duncan

Printed in Great Britain
by Amazon

10992753R00112